CW00865802

OTHEF
DARKNESS
AND OTHER STORIES

NICHOLAS VINCE

*By looking at
our own darkness,
we may understand
Other People's Darkness*

Nicholas Vince

Bibliofear

Bibliofear
13 Macclesfield Road
LONDON
SE25 4RY

First published in the UK by Bibliofear 2014

ISBN-13: 978-1495972164 (paperback)
ISBN-10: 149597216X (paperback)

CONTENTS

**For Craig
and those who waited.**

———

Acknowledgements

My sincerest thanks go to the following for their help in preparing this volume:

Marie O'Regan for her wise and encouraging editing.

Karen, Karen, Jane, Pia, Kathy and Sarah at the 'Book and Bottle' book club for the warmth and invigorating feedback on 'What Monsters Do'.

Tom Lucas for his insights into UK police procedures.

Carlos Castro for another creepy book cover.

———

For more information, and to contact
Nicholas and Carlos Castro,
please see:
www.nicholasvince.com

Facebook: **Nicholas Vince**

Twitter: **@nicholas_vince**

OTHER PEOPLE'S DARKNESS

It's amazing how seldom the world has ended. Though sometimes it feels as if it has. Like the time my best friend, Torrey, told me he was joining the army.

'You're doing what?' I said.

'I'm joining the army. You know, the people who defend the nation and your freedom to pass exams, stay on at school and go to university.'

We were standing in his bedroom in Streatham, South London. The afternoon sun was hot and we were dressed in t-shirts and jeans. He stood six feet tall and his shirt stretched over muscles; mine hung loosely.

'You are fucking nuts,' I said. 'You're sixteen: you can't vote, can't drive a car and you want to go off to Afghanistan or Iran or Iraq or whichever one it is and get yourself fucking killed? And for what? How does killing people over there make us safe in South London? Don't you remember how the London bombers said they acted because the fucking army was in Afghanistan?'

'It's not like I have much choice,' he said.

'What do you mean? We don't have conscription in this country. There are other jobs, you know.'

'Not without any qualifications.' He handed me his results statement. It was bad.

'OK,' I said. 'So, you can take them again. I can help.'

'I don't want your fucking help! You just don't get it, do you? I'm no good at this stuff. I don't want to end up stacking shelves—'

'You're not stupid, Torrey, but you're not thinking straight—'

'Do I have to punch you in the fucking mouth, to make you shut up?'

He moved closer, his fists clenched. He was a foot taller than me and I cowered.

'OK, OK. I'll shut up.'

He relaxed and sat on his bed.

'I'm sorry mate, I didn't mean … The army will train me and they'll help me get proper qualifications. I'll be out when I'm twenty-two.'

I nodded. 'Unless you get your fucking knob blown off.'

'Not thought of that.' He looked at me. 'You'll be OK, won't you?'

'You mean without you to stop the thugs at school from ripping my head off? Yeah. They're not staying on for A Levels.' I sat on the bed next to him. 'I guess the army gives you leave. I mean it's not like you're going to a war zone … oh, wait.'

He groaned. 'Stop now.'

'OK, OK. Shutting up. Weirdly, I'm quite proud of you. I still think you're a fucking idiot, but I'm proud of you.'

'That's you shutting up?' he said.

'Yeah, going home now.'

As I left the flat, I poked my head round the lounge door to say goodbye to his mum. She was watching daytime telly. People were screaming at each other and I don't think she heard me.

He left the next month. Me, my girlfriend Charmian, his mum and my parents; we saw him off at Kings Cross station on his way to Harrogate for army training.

His last words to me at the station were: 'You're not going to cry, are you?'

'Fuck off and look after your knob,' I said.

Nearly six years after Torrey joined up, on the evening of December 21st 2012, I stood in the rain on Streatham High Road.

When Torrey and I grew up there, the road was always congested with traffic, the pavements broken and shops boarded up with old sofas rotting outside. The street lights were dim or broken. The brightest colours were the yellow Metropolitan Police signs asking for witnesses to violent crime. It was once voted the "Ugliest Street in Britain".

Stretches of the road were dual-carriageway. In the central reservation was a brick flowerbed; two feet tall and about four feet wide, which the local council occasionally brightened with summer flowers. Most of the time it was mud and weeds.

I guess the aim of the flowerbeds was to encourage people to use the pelican crossings. Fat chance. People, school kids in particular, were and probably still are, terrifying drivers by dashing across the road where it suited them.

Early to meet Torrey, I stood in the rain as I didn't fancy sitting by myself in a pub. He was on leave from his posting in Helmand Province, Afghanistan. I'd missed him while he was gone, but was aware we'd grown up and grown apart. We hadn't met for nearly two years—his leave coinciding with my university term time.

He could leave the army or sign up for more. I wasn't sure which I wanted. So, I stared at a mural of Max and the Wild Things, in the rain, trying to decide. Because, obviously, it was all about me.

Even with my dawdling, I was in the pub on the High Road first. Just after six o'clock I rose to greet all six feet, two inches of Torrey. He looked great: tanned and with a short military haircut.

'So,' I said, as he gave me a hug, 'you still got your knob?'

He stepped back and laughed.

'Yeah,' he said. 'They give us *combat codpieces*. Good job, too. I'm seeing this girl, Drina.' He showed me pictures of her on his phone.

I told him I was still with Charmian and was going to propose to her on New Year's Eve. He insisted on buying whiskey to celebrate.

Torrey and I talked for nearly three hours and drank about five pints each on top of the whiskey. He said he was hungry and we agreed on a curry. It was a good meal, though he said I was a wimp for orderings a chicken korma, as he'd ordered the spiciest dish on the menu.

I had to ask him.

'Have you killed anyone?'

'Yeah … yes. I think so.'

'What you mean?'

'I'm a sniper, not like it's up close and personal. The targets are over a mile away.'

'Jesus. They really don't know what hit them, do they?'

'No,' he said and took a long drink of beer. 'I don't really talk about this.'

'I'm sorry, it was stupid of me—'

'It's OK, I want to. Can't think of anyone else to speak to.'

For once, I shut up and shared the silence until he spoke.

'I spoke to one of the veterans of the Falklands war. He said it was "shooting at smudges"; his targets didn't really look like human beings. He only knew if he'd hit the target if it dropped. But these days, with the advances in the scopes we use, they definitely look like people. But it's not like we go and take scalps or anything.'

He smiled at me. 'I think I'm tired of killing, but I do want to stay in the army. It's my home.'

I nodded and ordered another couple of beers.

When we finished the meal, we walked out of the restaurant and looked south to see if there were any buses heading north for Brixton, on the opposite side of the road. A number 159 bus was pulling away from the stop opposite the cinema. Perfect. If we cut straight across the dual carriageway, we'd catch it easily as it was gone eleven o'clock and there was little traffic.

He bounded ahead, and I expected him to leap over the flower bed in one go, but he stood on it and waited for me to catch up. As I got to him, he jumped onto the road, laughing at me for not catching him. I leapt after him.

The bastard in the black sports car must have been doing fifty miles an hour and he hit us both. I went up in the air and saw the night sky, which fell away from me. The next bit hurt.

I turned my head and saw Torrey lying on the ground.

Two blokes stepped off the pavement. They took one of us each. By the time mine got to me, I'd staggered to my feet but felt dizzy, so I sat on the brick wall of the flowerbed. Torrey was lying about six feet from me.

My bloke asked if I was OK and looked me closely in the eyes.

'We're doctors,' he said. I could tell: they were both calm. Other people were standing on the pavement, calling on their mobile phones—or filming us.

'How do you feel?' he said.

'Like I've just been run over.'

'Right. Stupid question.'

I looked across at Torrey. His lower legs looked wrong, twisted between the knee and ankle.

11

'Matt,' said the bloke kneeling by Torrey. 'You'd better come and have a look at this one.'

'I'm alright,' said Torrey. 'Once someone unties my legs, I'll be OK. I just need someone to untie my legs!' He wasn't angry; just very determined that someone needed to untie his legs so he could move them.

That didn't make any sense. No-one would have tied up his legs, unless they'd already got a splint on them. I tried focusing on Torrey and stood to walk over to him.

'It's alright Torrey, mate. These blokes, they're doctors.'

Next thing, I was back lying with my cheek on the road, thinking how cold and damp it was.

'He's awake,' someone said. I didn't recognise the voice.

I wished I wasn't awake as my fucking head hurt. Clearly I was in hospital as I could make out two nurses in the room with me. I tried to think of a joke about me being with two nurses. My mouth was dry and I couldn't speak.

'You're in hospital,' said one of them. I wanted to tell her I knew that.

'Your friend, Torrey, he's also here. He's in surgery at the moment and your parents and ...'

I closed my eyes as I was so tired.

'And he's asleep again,' said another voice. Charmian, I thought.

I woke up again, not knowing how much later, but it was still dark and I was so tired; too tired to open my eyes.

"What am I doing that's making me tired?" I thought. "All I'm doing is breathing. Right. So breathing is making me tired. So, if I stop breathing, then I won't be so tired."

I stopped breathing.

'We're losing him,' said one of the nurses.

I had my eyes closed and felt I was rising above the bed. When I opened my eyes, there was light. Bright light, but it didn't hurt my eyes. It felt like I was floating in warm liquid and moving towards the light. Utterly calm, utterly peaceful. I smiled. I grinned.

I heard a noise like *shush-taka, shush-taka*. Then I was back in the hospital bed and in pain and – after the floating – my body felt so heavy, as if I'd been beached; like gravity really, really worked and having lost control of me, wanted to prove a point. The light and warm liquid gone, the peace and serenity gone. The promise of answers—gone. It felt like the end of the world.

I didn't wake again until late the following afternoon and I asked about Torrey. They told me and I cried.

Torrey was really fucked up.

He kept his legs – and his knob – but he'd never walk without crutches. The army were kinda good to him, but it's not like he was wounded in battle. I mean it definitely wasn't our fault some joy rider was driving too fast up Streatham High Road; but we were drunk and didn't use the proper crossing. He soon found out he wasn't going back into the army on active duty. He was a bloody good sniper, but could hardly train others. Not really. However much he told me he could and I agreed with him, it just wasn't going to happen. I suggested they could find him an office job, that he could use his experience there, but he wouldn't listen. He kept talking about how he'd show the doctors, how there were things with stem cell research he'd heard about and he'd show the doctors, and everyone else, that he'd walk.

I was put on the general ward, with a lot of old blokes. Just being kept for observation. There was some shadowing on the scans of my brain.

Julian Cassidy, forty-nine years old, was in the next bed. He'd gone to his doctor scared he had lung cancer as he couldn't shake a cough. He'd smoked since he was thirteen. Doctor told him it wasn't cancer, but he did have pneumonia.

His coughing really hurt him, he went red in the face and grimaced with the pain. He was brave about it and didn't complain much. We talked about how the illness had made him really think about his life. He cheerfully told me about his wife and kids. And his mistress. Made me promise not to let on when his family visited.

'You know,' he said. 'That's it. No more fags, no more screwing around. I think this is what they call my moment on the road to Damascus. I've been a selfish bastard and I can really make a change now. I love my kids, I really do, and their mother. She doesn't deserve me mucking her around.'

I tuned him out when it struck me I'd had a life changing experience—and I felt nothing. Seriously. I'd been clinically dead for a couple of minutes and I didn't want to save the world, didn't feel I'd communed with God or had any more purpose than before. To be honest, all I really wanted was to go back. I missed being dead. No-one asks you to problem solve, or pay your bills, or buy a round when you're dead.

The next day, Cassidy was happier than I'd seen him since he'd arrived. The antibiotics he was on were obviously working.

After saying 'Good morning,' to him I turned to look at my cereal bowl and saw something out of the corner of my eye. Something about Cassidy's face had changed. It looked grey. I remembered something about going grey in the face being the sign of a heart attack and I buzzed the nurse.

As we waited for someone to come, I wondered if that was why I'd been sent back; I was here to save Cassidy. Perhaps he or one of his kids were needed to do something important and if he died, that wouldn't happen—and by being here, by calling the nurse, I had saved someone really important.

'What is it?' said Nurse Ratchett—not her real name.

'Cassidy, over there. I think he's having a heart attack.' He looked even greyer.

'No, I ain't,' said Cassidy.

The nurse looked at Cassidy and took his pulse.

'Where's the pain, Mr Cassidy?'

'What pain?' he said. 'I ain't got no pain. Not sure what's wrong with him,' he said, indicating me. 'I didn't ask him to call you.'

'But his face,' I said. 'He looks grey.'

'No he doesn't,' said Ratchett. 'If this is some kind of joke, Scott, then you'd … oh, never mind.'

She came over to me, shone a torch in my eyes, took my pulse. I pointed out I wasn't the one looking grey. She pursed her lips, made a note on my chart and walked away.

I looked at Cassidy again. His face was definitely grey.

I wondered if he was a vampire, or perhaps a zombie being treated on the NHS. That brilliant theory made no sense. As my doctor pointed out when I asked him about Cassidy, you can't treat those who're already dead. He assured me that these delusions about the other patients would probably disappear after a while.

I thought I hadn't explained myself properly. Cassidy was turning grey and they didn't notice. Cassidy himself, the doctors and nurses, no-one noticed. Eventually, I realised *I* was the problem. And no, I didn't fancy being shut up in a loony bin, so I shut the fuck up about it.

Grey isn't quite right. He was turning black and white, like he'd escaped from a 1930's movie.

After three days, the monochrome film effect had spread to cover him. In the morning, he got up to visit the toilet, insisting he was well enough to walk. His pyjamas, that I knew were red, were a rich light grey. He put on a dressing gown and that too became monochrome. As he walked down the ward away from me, it was like a TV or film effect. All of him was in monochrome, against the colour background of everything else.

When he got back to his bed he started coughing violently. I turned over in bed, away from him, and pulled the covers round my shoulders. I wasn't going to get involved. I might be hallucinating again.

He gasped for breath.

Silence …

He gasped for breath again.

I sat up in bed. The other blokes on the ward were looking at him. One shouted for a nurse and I wondered why he didn't use his bell push.

Cassidy looked at me. He was terrified. His eyes were flicking from side to side.

I got out of bed, crossed to him, looking for his bell push, thinking the nurse might not respond if I used mine.

'Nurse!' screamed the other bloke.

'Use your bell push!' I said to him. He looked offended I'd shouted.

Cassidy grabbed my hand. I expected him to hold it tightly, but he didn't have the strength. I covered his hand with mine.

'Can you see it?' I said. 'Can you see the light? Tell me!'

'Scott! Leave him alone and get back to your bed,' said Nurse Ratchett.

I dropped his hand.

'It's not my fault,' I said. 'I didn't …'

'I know,' she said. 'We'll help him now. Please, get back in your bed.'

They drew the curtains round him, but we all heard him die.

The week after Cassidy died they said the shadows on my brain had gone and I could go home. I went to see Torrey on his ward.

Drina was just leaving him and her mascara had run down her face. She didn't speak to me.

Torrey was lying in his bed, propped up on pillows, looking at the ceiling. When I reached him, I could see his eyes were red.

'Fucking dumped, huh?' I said.

'Yeah.'

'Blah, blah, better off without her, blah, blah, you'll get over it, blah, blah, good-looking cripple like you, you'll get sympathy vote, new bird in no time.'

He looked at me.

'Best you can do?'

'Not my strong point. I leave that kind of thing to Charmian. I can call her if you like.'

He looked at me and squinted.

'There's something different about you,' he said.

For a moment, I wondered if he'd gained the same power I had; that he was looking at me and wondering why I was turning grey. I glanced around for a mirror and he caught me looking.

'It's alright mate. It's not your looks, you're still as ugly as ever.'

I nearly told him, but I wasn't sure. I hadn't even told him about the near death experience. Like I said, I didn't want to talk about my new skill, gift, curse— hardly super power—as some bright spark might think I needed specialist treatment.

I smiled at him, looked him in the eyes and swallowed hard.

The pupils of his eyes were grey.

I tried moving my head to a different angle, checking this wasn't a trick of the light. I hoped I'd just become obsessed with the idea of people turning grey; that I was projecting this onto Torrey as I'd been upset by Cassidy's death.

Torrey snapped his fingers in front of me.

'Wakey, wakey mate,' he said. 'You OK?'

'Yeah. Just day dreaming. Listen, what are your plans for when you come out?'

'Living with Mum, until the council can sort out something for me.'

'I meant in terms of a celebration.'

He grimaced.

'You're going to organise something at the pub, aren't you? Well, fuck it. I don't want people—'

'Sorry,' I said. 'Can't hear you. Must be this head injury. I'm completely deaf to self-pity. You're getting out this weekend. You're going to meet people; your friends. I've asked your doctor, you can still get it up and fuck, so I—well, Charmian and me; we're going to find you a girlfriend. You are going to have children. You are going to fight this and beat it. You are going to live a happy and rewarding life. You are going to beat this. Do you understand me, Corporal?'

He looked slightly shocked, half smiled and then muttered. 'Sir, yes, sir.'

We hugged and I left him.

I spent ages stalking the corridors looking for his doctor. He assured me Torrey's injuries weren't life threatening and that he'd be out as planned on Saturday. So, it was just me then. Just me being stupid and imagining things about his eyes.

I didn't see Torrey the next day as I needed to make calls; organise things at work and for his homecoming party. Charmian went to see him and I asked her that evening about how Torrey looked.

'He's looking better,' she said. 'He's got some colour in his cheeks.'

I couldn't stop myself: 'What colour?'

'Uh, pink. You know, like people do when they're feeling better.'

On Saturday, Torrey's mum collected him from the hospital, so I didn't see him until that evening.

It was dark and raining as their car pulled into the pub's car park. His mum got out first and went to the boot to get the wheelchair. She opened the door and leaned in to say something to him. I couldn't see him, as I didn't want to rush forward, barge them out of the way and lift him like some prize from the back of the car. No, sorry, that's wrong. That's exactly what I'd love to have done. But it would have been a spectacle and I'm hardly built for carrying soldiers about the place.

So, I didn't see him until he was in the chair and had wheeled himself to the entrance of the pub.

People around me cheered, and pushed past to get to him and shake his hand. I just stood there, rain dripping down my face, mingling with the tears. I wiped my eyes with the back of my hand. Charmian was standing next to me, looking great. She had dark skin and curly black hair, with almond shaped eyes. She was dressed simply, didn't need masses of jewellery or makeup.

She took a couple of steps towards Torrey and realised I hadn't moved. She looked back and half smiled at me.

'What are you standing there for?' she said. 'Didn't I tell you he looked better?'

Not to me. He was turning black and white just like Cassidy, except when he got to me and I could see him under the light outside the pub, I could see his eyes properly. They weren't grey anymore. His eyes, all of his eyes; whites, iris and pupil were a dark brownish red— the colour of dried blood. I didn't understand what that meant. Cassidy had just gone monochrome, like in the movies, but Torrey looked as if someone had colourised his eyes.

He looked up at me, frowning.

'You look disgusted to see me, mate.'

I shook my head. 'What? No.' I smiled as best I could. 'No, it's just something in my eye. Come on, I've got your drinks lined up for you. You don't need to worry about driving home tonight … That didn't sound right.'

19

We moved to the bar, but I couldn't look at him.

He filled me with dread. I thought I knew what that meant. As a kid, I'd dreaded my father coming home from work to be told of my naughtiness by my mother; waiting for it to be weighed and punished. I'd dreaded being summoned to the headmaster's or the boss's office; but this was worse—it tightened my chest, made breathing hard. I couldn't tell him what I was seeing and I couldn't look at him. I went round the room, talking to people, asking if they'd spoken to him yet. I explained to everyone that they had to make sure they treated him as they'd always done, how that was important, how that would help him: how it might save him. I made sure everyone knew and that Torrey wasn't left alone for a moment, but every so often, I saw him looking across at me—saw his dark red eyes glistening at me and the expression on his face: the disappointment and accusation of betrayal.

Charmian spotted what I was doing and grabbed me by the arm.

'What the fuck, Scott? Why won't you talk to him?'

'You don't understand …'

She waited for me to go on, to say something miraculous which would excuse me. I couldn't. So I ran, pushing through people to get out of the pub. I knocked drinks and a table over. There were shouting voices, arms grabbing me which I shook off. Then I was outside and the freezing rain stabbed like needles as I fell on my knees in the car park and looked up to the sky and screamed.

Arms were put around my shoulders. I had my eyes closed, didn't really want to open them ever again. I felt Charmian's cheek against mine.

She must have been crouching as when I shook her free, and got to my feet, she went sprawling back, shouting my name.

'Leave me alone! Just fucking leave me alone,' I said.

Running from the car park, I hesitated, deciding whether or not I'd run onto the pavement or into the road in the hope some big fucking lorry would run me over. I remembered that being knocked down was what started this and who knew what would happen?

I walked on the pavement, beating my head with my fists.

I got home to my flat on Streatham Hill about six a.m, soaked through. I shivered from the cold, and the fear in the pit of my stomach; crouched in front of the gas fire, the water steaming from my clothes. Eventually, without standing, I stripped naked and curled up in front of the fire, too exhausted to attempt walking to the bedroom.

Around ten in the morning, someone banged at my front door. I didn't bother dressing before dragging myself to check who it was through the peephole.

Charmian looked at the door, knowing I was watching her. For a few moments I did nothing. She shook her head at the floor and folded her arms, exasperated.

I pulled open the door slightly and she pushed past me, ignoring my naked body. Figured.

She went straight to the kitchen and talked to me as she put the kettle on for tea, banging cupboards and tins; just in case I hadn't realised what deep shit I was in.

'You're an arsehole, Scott,' she said. 'Have I told you that recently? A fucking hypocritical arsehole. What did you think you were playing at last night? He's your best mate and you abandoned him. Not only that, you made it pretty bloody obvious the sight of him in his wheelchair disgusts you and you simply can't handle it.'

'It's not that,' I said.

'Then what?'

She looked me up and down. 'You stink, take a quick shower while the tea brews and then you can explain yourself.'

The shower did help clear my head. Once I'd dried myself, I dressed. As I did so, I realised Charmian hadn't changed her clothes since last night. That probably meant she hadn't slept as she'd been out looking for me. Uh oh.

When I joined her back in the living room, she sat on the sofa, holding her mobile phone. She was crying, huddled forward.

I sat on the sofa next to her and tried to put my arm around her, but she shook me off.

'This is so fucked,' she said.

'I know, I'm sorry, I shouldn't have run off like that, but you see—'

'Not you; Torrey, me, you. It's all just fucked up.' She turned to look at me. 'Torrey's dead. They found him this morning. He'd got himself up before his mum. He ran himself a bath and … and he knew he shouldn't do that … not on his own.'

We sat in silence for a few moments while I tried to work this out. Torrey had turned monochrome like Cassidy, but his eyes were different. Cassidy's were grey and he died a natural death. Torrey's eyes were dark red. Did that mean he'd committed suicide? Or just that he'd drowned?

Charmian stood.

'I've got to go,' she said.

Something wasn't right. I was missing something. Then it dawned on me and I stood up.

'What happened last night?' I said.

'What do you mean?'

'You said, *we* were fucked up. All three of us. Something happened. Tell me!'

I grabbed her shoulders and looked at her eyes. She was panicking.

'It was your fault,' she said. 'If you hadn't run off like that, not been able to face him. He was so upset … I just wanted to help him.'

'So, you weren't out looking for me last night.'

She looked confused.

'I didn't say I was.'

'No, because you were with him weren't you? What was it? Just to see if his knob still worked? Sympathy for the cripple? Or was it just something new? Something you could brag about to your mates?'

She brought her forearms up between mine and pushed me off her.

'So what? Which one of us were you jealous of? Him or me? The way you two went on, it's hard for me to tell.'

That was bloody ridiculous. Couldn't she understand blokes could love each other without wanting to fuck? I still blushed.

'Hah! It *was* him, you wanted him.'

I *wanted* her dead; just wanted her to shut up. My fingers flexed as I raised my hands to her throat to choke the voice out of her.

I froze. At first I thought someone must have entered the room and taken a flash photo as the pupils of her eyes went red. I blinked a couple of times to clear my vision, but her pupils were still bright fiery red.

'Get out,' I said.

She picked up her jacket from the back of the sofa and headed for the door. I kept my back to her until I heard her turn the front door handle, then span to face her. She was standing at the door looking at me. The red was spreading from her pupils and into the whites of her eyes. The other colours of her face and clothes were muted, washed out.

'Charmian, you're …'

What was I going to say? "I think you're going to die soon."

She left.

I paced the flat for ten minutes, then decided to start my laptop.

23

Wikipedia and Google weren't much help when I searched for "the colours of death". The sites I found explained how different colours denote death in different countries: some black, some white; or dealt with the stages of putrefaction. I did find a story about a cat in a hospice which snuggled up to those in their last hours of life. Really, no help at all.

There was a moment when I thought of telling someone, going back to the doctors, but they'd just put me away. I was sure of it. Or perhaps they'd want to experiment on me, work out what had happened to me.

Then I started wondering how I could exploit this gift. If there was some way I could sell my services to large corporations or governments as a freelance specialist; able to tell my employers when their staff and opponents would be dying. I could work in hospitals, could tell the staff who was about to die, so they could call relations; warn them and make sure no-one died alone.

And if that happened, would anyone ever speak to me again? They'd only ever have one question for me; "Am I going to die?"

Look, I know I was being ridiculous, not thinking properly; but my best friend had just died ... I mean, I might have just killed my best friend.

Charmian. The red in her eyes was spreading when she left. I'd wanted to kill her, but the thought had gone. I didn't really mean it, yet the red was spreading. Had I doomed her? Did I *have* to kill her?

I found my mobile phone and brought up Charmian's number. After looking at it for a couple of seconds, I touched the keys to delete it. Best if I never saw her again. A warning appeared asking if I was sure I wanted to delete her. I touched 'No'.

I called Torrey's mum, not knowing what I'd say and not wanting to spend time suffering, rehearsing the call.

'Hello?' she said.

I opened my mouth to speak but just wept like a teenager.

'Scott? Is that you?'

My chest hurt, I started panting between sobs. Jeez, I must have sounded like a pervert.

'I … I'm sorry,' I said and hung up.

I dropped the phone on the floor and stamped on it. I hurled things at the walls. Smashed things. I wanted to get hold of Torrey and slap him round the face, make him breathe, make him wake up and make him understand.

I grabbed a jacket and left the flat. I walked quickly and then started jogging, dodging pedestrians. I ran the mile to Brockwell Park and sprinted as far as I could before I fell to the ground, exhausted. I smelled dog shit in the grass and retched. I stood and stumbled away from the smell, as I couldn't stand the idea of someone asking if I was 'OK'.

I ambled round the edge of the park and through the fence I saw Charmian, on the other side of the road. She walked slowly, looking at the pavement.

There were some trees near the fence and I stood amongst them. The colour in her clothes and face were paler than when she'd left me an hour or so earlier. I guess she must have sensed me watching her, as she looked up and straight at me. Her eyes were a brighter fiery red. Whatever I'd started, it was still going to happen.

I ducked behind a tree and she walked on.

I wanted to be with her 24 hours a day as, if I wasn't going to kill her and her eyes were still red, then something else was going to happen to her and I had to be with her to save her.

She didn't return my calls. I went to her flat and sat on her doorstep, but I didn't see her.

On the Tuesday, at lunch time, Charmian called and we talked. Rather, she listened patiently as I explained I was a prat, and I was sorry, and I needed to see her to tell her what had really happened and how I'd known Torrey would die. I didn't want to say more than that over the phone.

We agreed to meet that evening, at nine o'clock in the pub. I shivered when I thought about how I was going to hold a conversation with her, looking into those red eyes.

At nine o'clock it was very cold and snow fell. Charmian wasn't in the pub when I arrived and I was about to order a drink when I realised I'd forgotten to get cash. I walked back out and was fumbling for my phone when I saw her.

She was walking down an alley opposite the pub. In the lamplight, I could see her clearly, a black and white image with glowing red eyes. When she reached a part of the alley without light, she hesitated, obviously nervous of the dark. She walked quickly through that area, and her body faded to a glow, leaving her red eyes shining brightly. She hurried to meet me, but she didn't hug or kiss.

'I've not got any cash,' I said. 'There's a machine just down the road, it'll only take us a couple of minutes for us to walk there.' I didn't want to leave her alone.

'If you think I'm spending another second out in the cold, you're wrong. You go get the cash and I'll get the first round.'

I hesitated.

'Well? Go on,' she said.

The pavements hadn't been gritted, so although it should have taken a couple of minutes to get to the ATM, it was closer to five, as I didn't want to slip and hit my head again. The machine was out of cash. The next machine was a good ten minutes' walk, so I called her on my mobile. When she answered, her voice was hushed and I could hear raised voices in the background.

'Charmian, it's me, look—'

'Scott. Stay away, there's something going on here.'

The phone went dead.

I hurried back, my feet slipping on the ice every few paces, but I didn't fall.

As I approached the pub, I could hear shouting.

I knew I wasn't going to die today. Earlier in the day, I'd stopped at a pharmacy and bought a small compact mirror. I'd been checking my eyes every couple of hours for the colours of death. Nothing, so I went with the theory that today at least, I was invulnerable.

There were screams from the pub and people were running out. I had to push them to one side to get in.

In the lounge bar two young men faced each other. A tall guy with his hair braided in cornrows was repeatedly pushing the other, with both hands, on the shoulders. Beside them, Charmian sat at a small table. She was still holding her phone and cowering.

'What you saying, man?' said Cornrows. 'That I can't talk to this bitch if I want to?' He indicated Charmian. 'She dissed my girlfriend.'

I assumed Cornrow's girlfriend was the one at the bar. She looked sixteen years old, and was clearly enjoying this.

'You this bitch's boyfriend?' Cornrows demanded of Smaller Guy.

'Actually, no,' I said. 'That's me.'

Charmian looked up at me. She was angry I'd spoken.

Cornrows swung round to face me. As he did so, he pulled a pistol from the back of his waist, under his jacket. He held it at arm's length, just above his shoulder, the barrel pointing down at my head.

'What you saying, man?'

'I said, I'm her boyfriend.'

Charmian stood and walked towards me.

'Scott, it's OK.' She looked at Cornrows. 'Please, I don't know what you thought I said, but I wasn't talking about your girlfriend … you don't need the gun.'

Cornrows looked at me.

'If he's your boyfriend, how come he's spending more time looking at me rather than you? Is he queer or what?' he said.

'Your eyes,' I said. 'I'm looking at your black, totally black eyes.'

'What you mean? They're brown, my eyes are brown!'

He pushed the barrel of the gun against my temple and I twisted away slightly under the pressure. All the time I was looking at his eyes. The black wasn't just in his sockets, but splattered across his cheeks.

As we stood there, waiting for him to make his mind up, he used the back of his hand to wipe his eyes free of the sweat dripping into them. To me, he looked as if he was crying darkness.

Charmian made a grab for the gun, but Cornrows swatted her away, turned and fired two shots into her face. He was turning the gun back on me when Smaller Guy smashed a beer bottle on the back of his head. He dropped the gun, but stayed standing.

I fell to my knees and held Charmian's hand, trying to comfort her. Stupid, stupid. She couldn't feel anything. He'd hit her in the forehead, and there was black stippling around the wound. The second shot was lower. Her nose was gone; the red flesh flowering around a hole in which blood bubbled for a few moments. Then silence.

I heard a beer tap dripping into a glass.

Cornrow's girlfriend screamed.

The police arrived a few moments later and caught Cornrows as he left the pub. He'd have got away if he hadn't insisted on dragging his girlfriend with him, shouting at her that this was all her fault and look what she'd made him do.

At the police station, I gave my statement—careful not to mention anything about knowing Charmian would die. I asked the detective why I hadn't moved.

Why hadn't I tried to stop Cornrows? I told him I could see every moment; it was all in slow motion. I must have had time to do something.

He said the slow motion didn't mean I'd had more time. It would all have happened in a couple of seconds. Literally, *two* seconds. Unless I was a trained soldier, I wouldn't have been able to do anything.

Torrey would have saved her.

I wanted to know if I could save people. For that, I needed a murder. So I headed for America. It wasn't much of a plan, as it was based on watching US cop shows and, to my British mind, insane US gun laws. Fly to America, wander around, look for people with darkening eyes, the serial killers, and try to stop them.

At Heathrow airport I wrote cards to my parents, Torrey's and Charmian's. I didn't know what to say, so I just told them I was going away and I'd be back if they needed me as a witness at Cornrow's trial. As I waited at the gate for the plane to load, I checked the other passengers. None of us was going to die soon.

It took me two minutes at a New York web café to realise how hopeless my plan was. High end estimates put the number of active serial killers in the USA at 300, out of a population of over 361 million Americans.

I thought of looking for the victims, but on the streets of New York I learned the fiery red eyes simply denote a violent death. It could be an opportunist mugging, road traffic accident or domestic violence. And if I stopped one of those, then how could I prove it was going to happen? Leave it to the very last minute and rescue someone? As I walked the streets, I thought it less likely. Compared to me, Americans are *huge* and I was convinced they all carried guns.

I thought of hanging around schools, looking for the dark eyed loner teen, surrounded by fiery eyed classmates. But there are thousands of schools.

So, I went to Kentucky and a town where people were bloodily dying. A serial killer targeted families and left them without their eyes. He killed them at the dinner table after drugging them – the police didn't say what he used, but they were awake – immobile and awake as he worked.

There was no pattern to the families he chose. People would have been less afraid if they knew their family wasn't on the hit-list.

The town had 3,632 residents, a handful of restaurants, a supermarket, a Christian university and no bars. It was completely dry. It had churches. Lots of them.

As I drove into town in a hire car, around three o'clock in the afternoon, I stopped to get my bearings. The main street was very quiet, with a couple of inches of snow and ice; the heating in the car was at full blast, drowning out the radio.

I fucking jumped in my seat when the guy behind me blared his horn. A TV news van swung round me and I expected to be shouted at as he went past, but the driver was concentrating on getting to the story.

I followed him for three blocks taking it more slowly, as I wasn't used to driving on the other side of the road and in snow. I pulled up as the cameraman and female reporter were getting out of the van. They joined two other news vans and some neighbours, standing in front of a house. A grey police cruiser had driven onto the lawn of what looked, to me, a very nice home.

It was a very nice neighbourhood and the nice neighbours had gathered to spit and curse at whoever came out of the house. The angry crowd grew. People arrived in cars and trucks. None of them carried a baseball bat or pitchfork, or a gun, as far as I could see. When people arrived, they looked curious, but after a few words with others the expressions changed, the muscles of their faces tightened to unblinking hatred.

A policeman was unrolling yellow tape across the front of the property. A couple more were holding people back at the driveway. As they were trying to deal with the reporters and the crowd the older one spoke into the walkie-talkie at his shoulder, asking for backup.

'Family Man! Family Man!' chanted a group of teenage boys sitting on the back of a pickup truck.

The news media sobriquet for the killer was ignored by the rest of the crowd until a man in his twenties was pulled onto the porch of the house. He had his hands cuffed in front of him and a policeman at either side. He looked confused, staring around him like he'd been woken from a deep sleep. There was a port wine stain covering the right side of his face. It wasn't smooth and I wondered why it hadn't been treated earlier, as it really disfigured him.

His mother was behind him, shouting his innocence.

The chant of 'Family Man' got louder and I had a queasy feeling in my stomach; this crowd was now a *mob* which might soon add the word *lynch*.

I wanted to get as close as possible to him, to see his eyes. I pushed my way between people's backs, after my polite English, "Excuse me's" were ignored.

They put him in a squad car on the driveway and a policeman, the sheriff, stepped towards the cameras to make his statement. Some of the crowd moved to hear what he was saying and others crowded the car with the cuffed man in it, so they could bang on the roof and shout at him.

As the car passed, he looked straight at me.

I was disappointed and frustrated. His eyes were clear, which meant I couldn't spot serial killers.

Turning from the drive I pushed my way past people and noticed their eyes. All of them had the darkness. Their faces were spattered with the ink dribbling from their eyes. They were going to lynch this guy if they got a chance.

The sheriff was obviously enjoying his time in front of the cameras. He said they had reason to believe they'd found the Family Man, but he couldn't comment further. Then he said that families could sleep easier tonight and gave a big grin to the cameras.

I started walking down the road away from the crowd, thinking how I could warn the oaf he'd better make sure his jail was secure, as this lot were coming for his prisoner.

A family were walking up the street towards me. Both parents dragged a toddler each, on a sled behind them. The parents were in their thirties. He was tall and had a craggy face, looking as if he worked outdoors. She was blonde and slightly plump.

I would have ignored them, but the father stopped me to ask what was happening. I couldn't speak for a few seconds, as I looked up into his eyes and then at his wife. Hers were the same and when I looked at the children I saw the fiery red in their eyes too.

It had taken me that long to work it out; the suspect's eyes were clear as the police had the wrong man. I was talking to the Family Man's next victims.

I explained about the guy with the port wine mark being arrested. The two little girls looked up at me and started giggling to each other.

'Girls, mind your manners,' said the father. He grinned at me. 'They think you talk funny.'

'Honey, I hope you don't mind me saying, but you look a mite peaked,' said the woman. 'Are you settled somewhere for tonight?'

'I was hoping to get a bed and breakfast and if not, then I guess I can drive back to Lexington.'

'There's no need for that, is there Tyler? We've got a fine spare room and we'd be happy to have you stay the night.'

I blinked a couple of times.

'Son, it's no use arguing with Winona,' said Tyler, his grin broadening. 'She does like finding strays and helping them back on the road. She regards it as our Christian duty to help strangers.'

'That's very kind,' I said. 'But, you don't know me. I mean, I may be ...' I looked down at the children, not sure whether I should mention the Family Man again.

'The Family Man? But you just said he'd been captured,' said Winona.

'OK, son. You'd best just give in,' said Tyler. 'You ain't going to find a room at this time of year. We've only got one Bed and Breakfast in town and there ain't no hotel.'

I agreed to stay the one night.

I'd found my victims and I wondered if Tyler had a gun and whether he'd show me where he kept it.

During our conversation, the red glowed more fiercely in their eyes and their faces became black and white.

I was given a generous sized bedroom and around six o'clock, Tyler and I retired to his den. The panelled walls were decorated with memorabilia of the sports he'd played in college. We quickly established that, I being British, we had nothing to discuss concerning baseball and American football.

I told him a very edited story of why I was here, mentioning only the accident, and the deaths of Torrey and Charmian.

I asked him about the Family Man killings.

'To be honest son, it's been real scary round here. People are still neighbourly, but they watch each other and there's been lots of talk. Mean, vicious stuff.' He stood up and walked to the bar and poured us both a small measure of bourbon. I raised an eyebrow when I saw the bottle. He smiled.

'You can't buy alcohol in this county, but there ain't a law against drinking it.'

He handed me my drink, then paced the room slowly without speaking for a few moments. I heard the ticking of a clock; I was running out of time.

'Real scary. I bought a gun a couple of days ago. First time ever.'

'A hand gun?'

'Yes. Couldn't believe how easy it was. Something wrong when it's easier to buy a gun than alcohol, don't you think?'

'Before I came here, I thought all Americans had guns,' I said.

He smiled. 'Cop shows.'

He walked to a set of books on the wall and took a key from his pocket, and unlocked a door in the false spines. I knew he was reaching for a gun and grew nervous. What if I was wrong? That he wasn't going to be a victim, but was a killer? As he turned towards me with the small revolver in his hand, the barrel pointing at me, I watched his eyes.

Bright fiery red. I was relieved, then sorry again.

He didn't hold the gun comfortably; like a child with an ice cream cone on a hot day.

'It feels wrong,' he said. 'They showed me how it worked at the store, but I don't know if I can shoot someone. I haven't told the girls we've got it.'

'Thou shalt not kill?' I said.

'That's right, but I've got to protect Winona and the girls. I got it hoping I can just wound him.'

'You don't sound convinced the police have the right man.'

'Like I said, there's been vicious talk. That Corey Dunstable, the neighbour they took?'

I nodded.

He said, 'He's ugly looking, but there ain't no harm in him. I'm sure of it.'

'Perhaps you should leave.'

"*Tonight. Now. Go,*" I thought.

'We've got family coming for Christmas and besides, I ain't running in fear.'

'But—'

'OK, you boys. Enough of your talking. Dinner's on the table,' Winona stood at the doorway and frowned when she saw the gun. 'Tyler. Put that away, the girls—'

'I'm doing it, I'm doing it.'

At the table, the eldest girl, Peyton, said grace—thanking God for food and their new-found friend. Her sister, Chloe, pulled faces and giggled.

'Will you take milk, or water or fruit juice with your meal, Scott?' said Winona.

'I won't, thank you,' I said. 'I was brought up not to have drink with my food. My dad said it dilutes the gastric juices. It means the food isn't digested properly.'

'That so? Well you learn something new, but in this family, we all take milk with our meals.' She looked at the girls. 'Good for growing bones, ain't it girls?'

The girls smiled and drank their milk.

Then the talk turned to who was ferrying the girls to school; which friends were going to a concert at the school tomorrow; who was picking them up and did they have phone numbers for the parents? Chloe's head fell forward into her dinner.

'What's wrong sweetie?' said Tyler. 'Long day at school, huh?'

He reached over and shook Chloe gently. Peyton slumped sideways. Winona reached to catch her, but, as she moved forwards, I saw her eyes flicker and she kept moving and fell to the floor, on top of the child.

'Tyler,' I said. 'It's the Family Man, he's coming here tonight.'

His eyes glazed and I had to stand to catch him.

Their eyes remained open and there was slight movement as they tried to swivel them to watch me. The red colour spread out of their eyes onto their cheeks.

I prayed I had enough time to carry the girls and drag the adults to their car.

I remembered which pocket Tyler had put his keys in, and was reaching into it when I heard the kitchen door creak open. I froze for a moment, then grabbed the keys and walked quickly to the door to the den. I would need that gun.

'Hello? Are you folks OK?'

I relaxed; it was a woman's voice.

'Can you call the police?' I shouted to her heading for the gun safe, as I still expected the Family Man. 'They've been drugged.'

I got the gun from the safe. Perhaps this neighbour would know how to use it, as I certainly didn't. Turning from the safe, back to the door, I realised she hadn't answered.

I thought guns should be cocked, so I pulled at the hammer, but it was really stiff. Perhaps if I just pointed the gun, that would be enough to scare him.

I held the gun up near my face, like I'd seen on cop shows, and I stepped quietly back towards the dining room. As I walked into the room, she had her back to me. She was wearing a big, thick padded snow jacket and stockinged feet.

She turned towards me. She was a big woman. What I'd taken for the padding of the jacket was all her and it wasn't fat. She was muscular and a couple of inches taller than me.

'There you are,' she said. 'I've called the sheriff.'

'I doubt that,' I said, pointing the gun at her.

She frowned.

'You're that guy's mother, aren't you?' I said. 'The one they think is the Family Man. No wonder you know he's innocent.'

The blackness in her eyes spilled in rivulets down her cheeks and onto her throat.

She held a small metal scoop in her left hand. The bowl was the size of an eyeball. In her right was a long knife, which I guessed came from Winona's kitchen.

I hoped I could keep her talking whilst I pointed the gun and reached for my phone.

'So, why did you kill them?'

She growled at me.

I turned on my phone, but realised I couldn't punch in the unlock code with just one hand as I didn't dare look away from her. Just keep her talking, I thought. Give myself time to think.

'You take the eyes,' I said. 'So something to do with the way they looked at ... at your son!'

'He looks different and they all made fun of him,' she said.

'Winona and Tyler? I don't believe you.'

'Not them, their girls! Evil little bitches!'

'They're children! For God's sake ... never mind. How did you do it?'

She snarled at me, but didn't move. I looked at the table. There was a plastic shopping bag, from the local supermarket. It held bottles of water, fruit juice and milk. I could see the top of a tabard under her jacket, showing she worked at the store.

'Got it,' I said. 'You drugged the milk. What? You watch who takes a special bottle?'

'Not so smart, are you? That would be too random. I pack their bags and if he's come crying to me and told me the things they say, then I say there's a leak in one of the bottles and go fetch another, special one.'

I edged towards the landline, which hung on the wall near the archway to the kitchen. She mirrored me, taking a step when I did and closing the gap between us. I stopped moving when she was about four feet from me.

'Close enough,' I said, indicating with the gun, that she should step back, but she kept approaching. So I pulled the trigger.

The bullet hit her in the shoulder and knocked her back a step. She staggered, but didn't fall. The knife dropped from her hand and bounced on the tiled floor at her feet.

'Oh God! I'm sorry,' I said. 'I didn't mean to ...' Seriously, I'm English, I couldn't help myself.

'Good Lord! That stings!' she said, rubbing her shoulder. 'Well,' she said. 'Are you gonna help me? Or just watch me bleed to death? I won't hurt you, honey.'

I was relaxing, but the black was gushing from her eyes, the rivulets covered her cheeks, hardly any skin visible. I stepped back and levelled the pistol at her again.

I caught sight of my face reflected in a glass fronted cabinet. My eyes glowed red. Fuck, fuck, fuck!

Shoot her again and possibly kill her? I couldn't.

I pointed the gun at the wall behind her and hoped the neighbours would report the shots to the police.

I pulled the trigger and the gun went 'click'. I tried again. Click. Click.

She grinned, stooped and picked up the knife in her good hand. She walked slowly towards me, enjoying the game of cat and mouse.

My backside touched the edge of a counter and I reached behind me. My hand found the metal handle of something.

She lunged at me with the knife and I brought the iron skillet around, aiming for her head.

I should have worried more about the knife.

She thrust it forward, into my chest, up near my arm. The aching, angry pain flowered and I panted, my breath difficult.

Fuck her! I wasn't going to let anyone hurt me. She thought she'd done enough and stepped back, but I took hold of the skillet with both hands and swung again at her wrist. She howled as the pan connected and I heard bones crack. I didn't stop, just swung the pan again at her face. It felt like hitting soft wood and the vibration rattled my hand. She swayed and then crumpled.

I didn't take my eyes off her as I dialled the police. A recorded voice said the number wasn't recognised. She groaned. I dialled again.

'Shit! You're the police! How can ...' I looked at a small card above the keypad. 'Idiot,' I said and dialled 911, rather than 999.

The sheriff didn't like me. He wanted to know why I'd almost killed the innocent mother of the Family Man. Charmingly, he conducted his interrogation whilst the ambulance people were dressing the wound on my chest—the knife had grazed a rib but hadn't penetrated further.

At the police station, he had me put in a cell. It became clear he didn't like the idea of being made to look foolish. Admitting he'd arrested the wrong man; that another family nearly died and an Englishman had saved the day—well, it just wouldn't do.

I wondered just how Kafkaesque this would get, until I remembered a phrase from those cop shows: "lawyered up". My lawyer established I hadn't been in the country when the earlier murders happened.

As I stood in the middle of the reception area with deputies applauding me, I smiled sweetly at the sheriff. He made it clear, hero of the hour or not, I wasn't welcome in his county.

Perhaps if he'd been nicer to me, I would have told him about his deputy. The one with the darkening eyes, who'd just seen the way his wife had smiled at his boss. I'd have told him about how he was turning more monochrome by the minute and of his fiery red eyes.

I walked out into the snow, without looking back, ashamed of myself.

Driving into Lexington I remembered the car needed a full tank of petrol when I returned it to the airport hire company.

The petrol station was busy, so I had to queue to pay at the counter. I had plenty of time to look at people's eyes, as they turned after they paid, and headed back to their cars.

'Hey, mister. You OK?' the girl behind the till said to me. 'Only you're crying.'

'I'm sorry,' I said. 'I'm fine. It must be allergies.'

Everyone's eyes were red. I didn't wait for my change, just ran to the car and drove to the airport. There were too many of them. Whatever it was, I wouldn't be able to save them.

As I approached the airline desks, to change my ticket for the next flight home, I realised it didn't matter. It wasn't just at the petrol station.

People around me are travelling all over the world. Looking into their eyes I can see it doesn't matter where I go, it will be the same.

The newspapers aren't any help, nor the news channels. Nothing about the end of the world. There's nothing to explain how it's going to happen—why the eyes of the children and elderly are all shining red and the rest have darkness weeping from their eyes.

I am not the cause of this. This isn't my fault. It's not a punishment for not warning the sheriff—it's not all about me. It's other people; *their* darkness.

Our darkness.

I fumble in my pocket for the mirror.

Will my eyes be red or black?

And which is worse?

HAVING ONCE TURNED ROUND

Gregory Payne watched the pack of four jam doughnuts on the table in front of him, waiting for them to miraculously fall to the floor or be cleared by the young woman who was diligently complaining to her colleague as she ambled around the tables in the motorway services, occasionally spraying and wiping them. After five minutes the girl glanced around the tables and told her colleague it was time for a break. Disappointed and elated, Gregory decided he'd have to open the pack.

The cellophane resisted tearing and crackled loudly. He paused, staring at the girls anxiously; these were supermarket bought doughnuts and he sat near a sign forbidding the consumption of anything but the overpriced food and drink purchased from the concessions. If he'd been here with Nathalie and their three sons he'd have felt justified, but alone he felt the transgression keenly.

Eating just one doughnut out of four wasn't in his nature, so he decided to eat *just* two. Lifting the first he found the red hole which showed where the jam had been pumped inside and bit through the soft dough. The jam covered his tongue and evoked a guttural grunt of pleasure. He took a paper serviette and wiped his mouth. The smear of red jam on the white paper, amongst the granulated sugar from the coating, was too red for blood; but it reminded him of the murder of love he was going to commit that weekend.

Except, of course, there would be no blood, no cathartic violence. He'd poisoned his marriage for weeks now, administered via doses of passion with Alex; the lover from whose lips he'd licked strawberry jam and sugar the previous week.

Gregory quickly finished the first and second doughnuts and regarded the third. Again, he looked round to check no-one was going to disturb him and lifted it to his mouth. The biting of it was more than an act of remembrance for passion: it was defiance. By taking a third, he was proclaiming his freedom, his adulthood, his right as an individual to behave as he chose, to be greedy; in spite of common sense, and in spite of any promises he'd made to himself and Nathalie about his weight.

The taste of jam and sugar filling his mouth brought back the sensation of Alex's jam sweetened tongue in his mouth, and he moved his left hand to his pocket to stroke his stiffening cock. He blushed as he realised he might be seen and quickly put both hands flat on the table, taking two deep breaths to calm himself.

There was a mirror opposite him, on the back of a concession stand. Bad move on the part of the interior designer, he thought. It probably gave a sense of more space in the seating area, but tired travellers didn't want to see how wrecked they looked. From this distance, Gregory could see bags under his eyes and the fact he should lose half a dozen pounds. Blaming Nathalie's cooking wasn't fair. At thirty-nine, he could do more exercise if he chose, but the truth was it was easier to let himself go, to drown in the charnel dust of his life.

The bleakness of the metaphor surprised him, but it was true. He didn't hate Nathalie, but he no longer loved her and the daily boredom of his marriage was suffocating him. The boys were teenagers, and within half a dozen years all three would have gone to university and he'd be left with Nathalie; their home a dusty mausoleum. The joke was, he didn't want to leave them. His life was comfortable and part of him wanted to end the affair. Choking he may be, but life with Nathalie and the boys was familiar and safe. The affair, like his craving for doughnuts, was inconvenient.

Clearing his throat he looked more closely at his face in the mirror. He decided he was still handsome, his trimmed goatee and cropped dark hair worked with his brown eyes. Smiling slightly, he winked at himself and looked down at the table.

He was full, but the last doughnut sat in front of him. He looked around for the bin, as eating it would be just pure greed. On the other hand the doughnut appeared ridiculously lonely; there was nothing wrong with it and Nathalie hated wasting food at home, so he ate it and felt slightly nauseous as he swallowed the last mouthfuls.

The paper serviettes still left his hands sticky, so he went to the toilets to wash his hands and face. After he'd dried his hands, he entered a cubicle intending to piss. Although – miraculously – it was clean, suddenly there was phlegm at the back of his throat. He choked, gasping breaths for a few moments and vomited up a couple of gobbets of doughnut. He wanted to believe it was just the speed he'd eaten, but knew it was a sign of his fear and excitement about the weekend with Alex—and his guilt. Obviously his guilt, and mourning for Nathalie's love and that of the boys, which he knew he'd lose if he left them.

After retching, he took a piss, washed and dried his hands again, and walked slowly back to his car through the heavy October rain.

In the car he reflected this was the longest journey he'd made to see Alex and decided that's why he was gagging afraid. At work, he'd be busy up till the moment he'd head for Alex's flat—a ten minute walk. He had only a few minutes of conflicting anticipation and regret to deal with, but this weekend meant a journey to Wales and hours in the car. He licked his lips, hoping to find a smear of jam or sugar he'd missed, to remind him of the delights he was driving to.

The weather cleared as Gregory drove into Merthyr Tydfil to meet Alex at the train station.

They strolled around the shops happily, until Alex reached to grasp his hand on the street. Gregory froze. Alex frowned at him.

'For God's sake,' Alex said. 'It's 2014. I know it's Wales, but I'm sure they have queers here too.' He drew breath to continue, but saw Gregory's face. 'OK, OK. No holding hands for fear of frightening the locals, and horses if they have any.'

They walked on until they found the restaurant Alex had booked for lunch.

After they'd ordered, Gregory looked at Alex in the sunlight. Unlike Gregory, at the age of thirty-nine, he still had a dancer's physique. Long blonde hair swept back from his tanned face and blue eyes.

Gregory leaned forward and took his hand.

'I'm sorry about earlier. This is all strange, OK? I mean, I remember what it was like before, years ago, but … look I just need time.'

Alex lifted Gregory's hand to his lips and kissed it gently.

'I was thinking about the time thing. How does the rest of our lives sound to you?'

Gregory flinched and Alex released his hand. Alex smiled slightly.

'Too long, eh? I am serious. I will divorce Brian.'

The waiter arrived with their food. Alex had ordered a salad and he grinned as he saw Gregory's discomfort when presented with a large plate of roast beef, with considerable trimmings.

'Not thought of myself as a chubby chaser, but you know that doesn't matter. Enjoy your meal,' Alex said.

'I'm on holiday and I'll comfort eat if I want to.'

'I'll take one of your roast potatoes to lighten the load.'

The lunch stretched on longer than they'd originally planned, as eating was repeatedly interrupted by laughter. They talked of their time together at dance school, friends and the recent school reunion and their first brief affair, during their last year at school.

Every so often Gregory would grow quiet, as his heart thumped in terror of the one thing he truly feared, the thing which meant change from the comfortable lie he was living—he was falling in love with Alex.

In the car park Alex insisted they stick to their original plan of driving north through the Brecon Beacons, so they could enjoy the scenery. Gregory pointed out they wouldn't see much, as it would be dark in an hour. Alex pulled a face of exaggerated disappointment.

'Your mouth looks sad,' Gregory said. 'Let me kiss it better.' They kissed and Gregory wished he'd saved at least one of the donuts.

As they drove into the national park, the sunset was magnificent on the mountains. But it was brief. Soon they were driving the narrow roads in the dark. Bounded by high hedges or stone walls on either side, most of the bends in the road were blind.

'Perhaps it wasn't such a good idea to put "shortest route" into the sat nav,' said Gregory. 'God knows what we do if we meet someone coming in the other direction, there aren't any passing places.'

'Well, they'll have their headlights on. You'll see them in plenty of time.'

'What if they're broken down and their lights don't work, or if it's a tractor and it's got one of those forklifts? We'll drive onto the spines; they'll come smashing through the windscreen.'

Alex thought about this.

'It's the cannibals you want to worry about.'

'What?'

'They leave bodies in the road, and when you get out to see if you can help, that's when they jump on you. And don't stop if you hear a thump on the roof of the car.'

'Why not?'

'Everyone knows it'll be a lunatic with a head in a bag, which he's banging on the roof.'

Gregory's hands tightened on the driving wheel and he hunched forward, peering ahead. The rear view mirror was black, as there was no car behind them. That made him more nervous, as he'd seen a TV programme as a kid; where a hooded skull suddenly appears in the mirror, causing the driver to crash.

The road crested a hill and as they headed down into a valley, the only habitation they could see were the lights of a house, three or four miles away on the other side.

Soft rain fell, making the road slick in the headlights. Gregory set the wipers to intermittent. A big cat, a panther Gregory thought, landed on the bonnet and roared at them. The howl was deafening. Gregory braked hard and the car skidded, hitting a tree. The airbags smashed into their faces as they were thrown forward.

Darkness.

When Gregory came to, he realised there was more than one cat creature. Panther wasn't right as the ears were wrong and they didn't seem to have fur, just grey skin. They prowled just outside the remaining headlight beam, so he only glimpsed them, but their growling breath gave him an idea where they were. The ammonia smell of their urine stung his eyes. He thought there were three of them nearby, and wondered if there were others.

He coughed violently as he inhaled some of the powder from the airbags and struggled to catch his breath. One of the creatures landed on the bonnet again, silhouetted against the light, and rocked the car. It punched through the shattered windscreen. Claws raked across his cheek and his coughing became deep gasps for air.

The seatbelt released easily. He wrenched open the car door and was out and backing away from the creature, stumbling and not caring about the others. He just wanted to be away from it.

He turned from the car and searched for the lights they'd seen earlier. The house was visible above a wood on the other side of the road. He ran through the trees, and lifted his forearms in front of his face to ward off the branches which whipped his eyes.

Moments after Gregory left, Alex woke and could taste his blood trickling into his mouth from a bloodied nose. Disorientated, he couldn't get the seat belt to release and after a few moments struggling, he fell back in his seat. The growling became loud purring.

Gregory stumbled through the woods for five minutes and slumped against a tree, coughing, his lungs burning. His chest and throat were sore and his shoulder, where the seatbelt had held him, felt bruised. The coughs became sobs of fear.

He remembered Alex and looked behind him for the headlight, so he could navigate to the car. It had failed and he had no idea how to get back. The light from the house was his only option. He listened for movement in the bushes or a low growl.

The woods thinned the closer he got to the house, but he still tripped over a root and fell hard to the ground. The pain in his shoulder changed from ache to agony. He crawled a few paces before he was able to stand and walk to the edge of the road, where he could see the house forty feet above him on the valley wall.

He listened for the cat creatures for over a minute before stepping onto the tarmac and was suddenly fearful a car without lights would mow him down.

The rain clouds broke, revealing a full moon. By its light, he saw a small lychgate set in a dry stone wall and a path rising through a garden to the house.

The effort of climbing the shallow steps hurt his thighs and hips. He approached the front door and a security light flashing on startled him. The house looked old, as the walls were made of stone and the door was dark and ancient wood. There was no bell push, so he used the large iron knocker. It was absurdly loud and he was scared it would attract the cat creatures. There was no answer.

To his right, a path led from the front door round the side of the house. There was no gate, so he decided to follow it. Another security light came on at the corner of the house, showing a semi-circular patio made of brick. The patio doors were open, and a breeze lifted net curtains out from the dark room beyond.

As he stepped forward to enter, his car horn sounded. Retracing his steps, he came to the front of the house and looked down into the valley. Clouds covered the moon and it was too dark to see beyond the security light. The horn stopped and he waited for it to sound again. He shifted his weight nervously, listening.

Bushes rustled in the garden, but he wasn't sure if that was the wind or the creatures. The cold chilled him and he turned back to the house, scanning the upper floor for a light, hoping the residents had been disturbed. Using the knocker again, with his body weight behind it, still produced no response.

Leaving the front door, he hurried back to the patio and looked up at the dark windows on that side. The patio doors were still open and he walked into the house.

It occurred to him that one of the creatures might have already entered, while he was around the front of the house. If he closed the doors, would he be shutting the monsters out? Or had one or more already entered and he'd be locked in with it … or them?

He held his forehead in both hands, and smoothed them backwards over his hair, whimpering quietly. He couldn't hear the creatures and decided to close the doors.

He pushed at the door nearest him, but it didn't move. Tears blurred his vision. He used the back of his right hand to wipe them away, so he could look for a lock. There was nothing visible, so he ran his fingers up the edge of the door to feel a latch. Nothing.

Crouching slightly to get his bulk behind his shoulder, ignoring the pain and hoping a different angle of force meant the runners would work smoothly, he tried the door again. The door juddered in its tracks, but it did close. The second door moved under the same technique.

Straightening up, he turned to face the room and wondered if the owners were likely to shoot an intruder. This was an isolated part of Wales. To his Londoner mind, it was possible—actually, it was probable.

His chest tightened and breathing became harder and louder. He realised that wasn't good. He might be having a heart attack and his breathing, which was all he could hear in the room, would attract the owner; who he was now convinced would use both barrels of a shotgun on him.

'Hello, is there someone there?'

Her voice came from the shadows at the far end of the room.

'Please, answer me. I heard noises outside. Wait a moment, I'll find the light.'

'No!' His voice was louder than he meant. 'No,' he whispered. 'They'll know we're here.'

She made a small cry.

'What do you mean? What are you talking about?'

'Some kind of ... big cats, I think. They attacked us, my friend. We've got to get help. Your phone, where's your phone?'

'I've already called the police from my bedroom. They're on their way and they'll be here in about twenty minutes. But, your friend? Should I call an ambulance? Can we help him?'

'No! ... no, I think it's too late for that and I don't know I if can find the car.'

He heard her sigh in the dark.

'So, the truth is: your friend is injured and you're too scared of whatever it is that attacked you to help him.'

He worked his jaw a couple of times and ran his tongue over his lips.

'I didn't want to come here, it's not my fault. It was his idea, all his. Look, do you have a drink? A brandy, whisky, anything?'

'Yes, but can we at least put on a table lamp? I don't want you to crash into things in the dark.'

'I guess so. Look, I'm sorry, this is your home and I've ... Gregory, my name is Gregory, what's ...?' He faltered as the table lamp was switched on and he saw the shelves.

From floor to ten foot high ceiling, there were small cubby holes between four and twelve inches across. He thought there were hundreds, then realised it must be thousands. No two were the same size as they looked to be bespoke for the contents. In each was an object, and a stand to display it. Small things: key-rings, wallets, gloves, lipsticks, purses, mobile phones; the sort of things we all carry. He turned slowly, trying to take it all in and then half smiled as he spotted a small ball of rubber bands. His mother kept one of those in a kitchen drawer.

'Excuse me, but what are all these?'

'Gifts. Mementoes. I am called Miss Elspet.'

He decided she must be in her eighties. Her hair was white and beautifully sculpted above high cheek bones and deep violet eyes. She wore a dark orange lambs wool sweater, with a pearl necklace, and a tweed skirt.

She sat in a wing back chair, holding an ebony cane with a silver handle, and inevitably, he thought of Dickens' *Miss Havisham*. She looked so frail and there was a visible layer of dust on every shelf and object.

'You look as if you need that drink. You'll have to pour it yourself, I'm afraid. The cabinet is over there.' With a slow lift of her cane, she indicated a 1930's wooden drinks cabinet.

He took a couple of steps towards it before he stopped and turned back to her.

'I'm sorry,' he said. 'Do you want a drink?'

'There's sherry there, I think.'

'And your name, you told me and I've already forgotten.'

'Miss Elspet.'

He poured the drinks and passed the sherry to her. She indicated he should sit in the chair to her left, on the opposite side of the table which held the lamp.

He raised his glass. 'Here's to new friends.'

'And here's to old friends. What is your friend's name?'

He looked at his glass, not her eyes.

'Alex.'

He said the name quickly, before downing the rest of his brandy.

'Take another,' she said. 'I think you need Dutch courage.'

He flinched at her scolding tone, but rose and went back to the cabinet, holding his glass tightly. He poured himself another large measure of brandy.

'Can you remember ever being brave, Gregory?'

The question shocked him. He thought hard. It was ironic; he remembered he'd once fought monsters.

'When I was a kid, I played at fighting monsters with my mates. We were always the heroes, the Dr Whos of our universe; which extended from The Town Park Nebula to The School Playground Galaxy. I fought nameless things; things with tentacles and teeth; things which hid in alleys and leapt to chew our little sisters and steal our mothers.'

He smiled into his empty glass and filled it again.

'You see? I fought and beat countless monsters—until it was their turn to win.'

As his eyes adjusted to the dim light from the table lamp, he could see her more clearly. Her white hair had strands of dark and there was a fullness to her lips he hadn't noticed before.

'And your friend, when did you meet?'

'At dance school. We lost touch, but we met again recently.'

'And you fell in love with him.'

He looked at her sharply, suspicious she might be judging him, and wondered how she knew. She was smiling kindly.

'I don't want to talk about this.'

'You should, you know. People will want to know why you left him to die. You'd better get your story straight.'

He looked at the glass in his hand and finished the drink. As he tried to put it back on the cabinet, he thought of interviews with the police and his hand shook.

'You're right,' he said. 'I shouldn't have left him. But I came to get help, didn't I? I found you.'

He put his glass on the cabinet, and wondered if he should offer to wash it.

'I'll go,' he said.

'There's a torch by the front door, you'll need a torch.'

'What? Yes, thank you, I'll close the door, but please don't lock it. I'm sorry, that was rude. You'd better call for that ambulance.'

He found the torch and checked it was working. Stepping into the cold, dark and damp; he pulled the door closed behind him, ensuring it was on the snib, to prevent it locking.

The path leading from the house to the road was steep and he hoped Alex had recovered enough that he could walk up, as he knew he couldn't carry him.

He didn't want to attract the attention of the cat creatures, so he shone the torch briefly and relied on memory of what he'd seen of the path.

At the road, he looked across into the woods he'd run through earlier. He had no idea of how to find the car on the other side of the trees, and he could reasonably claim to be unable to return to the car, but he was now more concerned about Alex. Perhaps it was just the brandy, but he was determined to save him.

Through the trees, he saw the glow of fire, low down on the ground. The thought of Alex burning to death sickened him.

The fire was real and he could deal with this. Whatever he'd thought earlier, whatever he'd imagined he'd seen, must have been tricks of the light; something natural. Perhaps their silly conversation about cannibals had spooked him more than he'd thought.

But there had been a large cat, he was sure of it. He found a thick branch on the ground to use as a weapon.

Pushing through the trees, he had no choice but to use the torch more as he was scared of tripping over a tree root and smashing his head.

He thought of what Elspet had said; how he needed to get his story straight for the police, and Nathalie. This was the first time he'd really thought about her since the accident. Just as long as Elspet played along with his story of coming to her for help. Or if she couldn't speak; if he silenced her. He shuddered and stopped walking as he thought about this. The branch in his hand could be used on both cats and her.

No, he'd pay her money so she'd support his story.

Except, she'd already called the police, when she heard him in the house. He'd have to explain the timings. And he had no idea how much he'd have to pay her or how he'd explain the missing money to Nathalie. The lies were becoming too complicated to handle and for that reason, he decided to be honest: he'd been scared and confused, thought Alex needed help he couldn't give him and so he'd run. That was his story.

Stopping to get his bearings he realised he was walking in the wrong direction. He'd been concentrating on the ground and avoiding tripping over roots, and now the glow from the car was over to his right. It was still four to five hundred yards from him. He walked towards the fire, dread quickening his pace as he wanted to confirm, or deny, his fear of seeing Alex's burned remains in the car.

He pushed that picture from his mind with the image of a photo of them from dance school. They'd danced a pas de deux, as part of an end of year show. Alex was taller than he was and during the routine, he'd lifted Gregory above his head. He had a black and white photo of the moment in his jacket pocket. He'd intended giving it to Alex as a memento.

"Mementoes," she said all those things were mementoes. Of what or who? Of course, cannibals kept trophies from their victims and Gregory wondered if they'd call them "mementoes". Great, now he was obsessing about the story Alex had told in the car.

He stumbled against a tree, hurting his shoulder. Panting, he looked around to get bearings. He was still amongst trees, about a hundred feet from the car.

The petrol tank in the car exploded. The heat washed across his face. Hesitating for a moment, he ran towards it, desperate to save Alex. Standing on the tarmac, he squinted against the heat into the passenger seat. It looked as if the car was empty. He leant forward, hands on knees, to catch his breath. Faintly, he heard a wolf whistle. He straightened and scanned the road. About twenty yards further down the road Alex was sitting on a bank, with his back to a tree, smoking a cigarette. The cat creatures had gone.

Gregory walked towards him, thinking what to say. As far as he could see, by the light of the burning vehicle, Alex wasn't hurt. His brown, hooded jacket was torn in places and his hair was matted and face dirty.

'I'm sorry about your car,' said Alex as Gregory joined him.

'It wasn't your fault.'

'Yes it was.' He looked Gregory in the eye. 'I didn't like sitting alone in the dark and I thought fire would keep *them* away, and I've always wondered what it would be like to blow up a car.' He indicated the stream of petrol running down the road, which he'd used as a fuse.

'You fucking blew up my car? What am I going to tell Nathalie and the kids?'

'I honestly have no idea what you're going to tell your family. I suppose the truth is out of the question?'

Alex watched Gregory, waiting for an answer. During the silence he rubbed his left shoulder.

'I thought not. Where have you been?'

'To get help.'

Alex looked dramatically up and down the empty road.

'So you didn't just run from whatever it was that jumped on the car?'

'What the hell do you take me for?' Gregory looked down. 'I'm sorry, I was scared.'

'There's hope for you yet … hope for us. Did you find help?'

'Yes, there's a house through the forest. A nice old lady … can't remember her name … anyway, she's called for the police and an ambulance. Can you walk?'

'Which way?'

'Well, I came through the woods. It's about ten minutes. There's a house on the other side of the valley.'

'You mean that one?' Alex pointed up the road. It was about half a mile from where they were. They could see the lychgate.

'The bend in the road, the trees ... I didn't see.'

'OK, help me up,' said Alex.

Dropping the branch he'd found, Gregory put Alex's left arm around his shoulder. As Alex got to his feet, he suddenly sagged and Gregory had to hold him.

'Feel faint,' said Alex.

He swayed for a few seconds, blinking rapidly.

'OK,' he said. 'That's better. Just got up too quickly.'

They got down the bank and when they reached the road, Alex said: 'Ouch, that hurts.'

'What does?'

'My stomach, to the left.' He massaged his belly and reminded Gregory of his eldest son, reporting a fall from his bike.

'Well, the sooner we get help the better,' said Gregory. He studied Alex's face as best he could, using the torch. It was difficult to see if he was pale.

'Did you try using your mobile phone?' said Alex.

'What?'

'Did you try using your mobile phone? Small marvel of modern technology. I don't have a signal.'

'I deliberately let it run out of juice. It has a tracking app on it, so Nathalie can see if my train's delayed. I didn't want her knowing where I was in Wales.'

They walked on.

After a few paces, Alex groaned. 'Bloody shoulder,' he said.

Gregory remembered something about keeping crash victims talking, so you could judge ... something or other.

'Talk to me,' said Gregory.

'What about?'

'Anything. Recite a poem, but I need you to talk to me.'

Alex thought for a few moments, then looked behind them. Gregory, wanting to keep momentum, looked ahead into the torch beam.

'"Like one who on a lonely road,
Doth walk in fear and dread."'

'Cheerful.'

'I was being subtle, as I don't know if he … it, can understand English.'

'What?'

Gregory listened and heard the low growling. He turned round. The creature was silhouetted against the burning remains of the car.

It was devoid of fur and sat on its haunches, around six feet tall. Wrinkled grey skin covered its emaciated body, except for the pink hands, the fingers of which ended in glinting black talons. A cat's face, with large bat-like ears, snarled to show thin sharp teeth.

At first Gregory thought its eyes glowed from the reflected light from the torch, but when he dropped the beam, they burned as if its skull was full of flame. A long skinny tail was wrapped around its torso and it idly played with the end.

It was about ten feet from them and that felt like springing distance, as it dropped to put its front paws on the ground.

'Nice kitty,' said Alex.

The thing cocked its head, as if listening. They took a step away from it.

'Vile, disgusting, scary kitty,' said Gregory.

It stretched one forepaw on the ground closer to them, in a stalking pose.

'I suggest that we walk away slowly,' said Alex.

'Agreed.'

They'd taken a half dozen steps before another of the creatures leapt over the hedge at the side of the road ahead of them. They froze as it walked on all fours, past them to join the other.

'Ah, twins,' said Alex.

'I think there's another,' said Gregory. On cue it bounded over the hedge on the other side of the road and joined its companions.

Gregory and Alex looked at each other and silently agreed to carry on walking towards the house.

The creatures purred, their feet moving silently.

'Please don't feel it necessary to point out that cats like playing with their food,' Gregory said. Alex grunted.

'How's your shoulder?'

'Painful.'

'You don't think you're having a heart attack do you?'

'I don't know. I've never had one. But, yes, the thought had crossed my mind. The pain's worse here.' He rubbed his belly again, on the left side, below the ribs.

They spoke quietly, as they didn't want to annoy the cats.

They reached the path to the house and one of the creatures bounded past them to the road beyond, and stood its ground.

'Ah,' said Alex. 'We're being herded.' He looked up at the house. 'Your old lady friend; she didn't bid you welcome and invite you to "enter freely and of your own will," did she?' Gregory said.

'What's that?'

'A Dracula joke.'

'No, she didn't.'

All three creatures growled and moved to circle them, then approached a couple of steps, obviously impatient.

Gregory opened the gate and they walked up the path. Alex swayed again, so Gregory wrapped his arm around his chest to support him.

They could hear the creatures shadowing them in the bushes.

'Fuck,' said Alex, rubbing his belly every couple of steps.

Gregory reached for the handle on the front door but a hiss from one of the creatures stopped him. They were herded round the house, back to the patio doors. Gregory felt safer in the patio light, until he turned to see three pairs of glowing eyes watching him from the bushes. For a moment he was convinced the door would be locked and if he looked hard enough at the patio, he'd see blood stains on the bricks.

The patio door slid open and a woman stood aside to let them in.

'Come in boys,' she said.

Immediately, three normal size Sphinx cats tumbled past them and clambered to lie on the tops of chairs and the sofa.

'Take your friend to the spare bedroom. It's through there.'

She indicated a door at the far end of the memento room.

Inside the bedroom, Gregory supported Alex and sat him on the edge of the bed.

'Jesus Christ, that hurts!' Alex said.

In the light of the room, Gregory was shocked at how pale he was.

Alex shook off his jacket and pulled up his sweatshirt. He looked down at his belly then at Gregory. There was a swelling below the ribs on the left side, with an ugly bruise.

'Brian, I can feel a swelling here.'

'Alex, it's me, Gregory. Remember? Brian's away in Geneva. That's why we're away this weekend.'

Alex frowned.

'Gregory? From dance school? I loved you then. Always have. Did I tell you that? I feel dizzy, Gregory. Gonna throw up.'

He leaned forward and was as good as his word. Gregory leapt back, avoiding the vomit, but the carpet was a mess. Alex fell back on the bed. His eyes were moving rapidly from side to side as he tried to focus on Gregory.

'Wait here,' said Gregory. 'I'm going to get the owner; I'll get her to find out how soon the ambulance will arrive.'

Gregory went back to the mementoes room. As he entered, the three cats got up and pushed past his legs, through the door. The woman sat in the wing back chair. The ceiling light was on and Gregory could see her more clearly. He stared at her.

'Didn't your mother teach you it's rude to stare?' she said.

He wasn't sure if he was speaking to the same woman he'd seen before. He remembered her as being in her eighties, but this woman was in her forties at most. She was more motherly than he remembered. It must be the elderly woman's daughter.

'I'm sorry … my friend, he's been sick and I was wondering if I could phone the ambulance again, to see how long they'll be. I mean I'll clean up the room.'

'Is your friend very ill?'

'Yes, I think he is. Look, can I use the phone?'

'The phone's not working. I told you that before. Don't you remember?'

'What? No. You said you'd called for the police and that you'd phone for an ambulance.'

'I'm sorry, you must have misunderstood. I assumed you had a mobile phone. I'll go through and look at your friend. I may be able to help him. If not, then I can drive us to the hospital—there's one in Brecon. Fix yourself a drink, there's brandy in the cabinet.'

'Your name,' he said.

'I told you before, you silly man, it's Elspet.'

She left Gregory and joined Alex, stepping carefully over the puke on the floor. She looked at him critically and closed the door.

'There isn't much time, the ambulance will be here soon,' she said. 'Quickly, tell me your story.'

'What do you mean?'

'Tell me how you met, Gregory, I just enjoy a good love story.'

Alex snorted and looked at her. Well, if it took his mind of his pain, why not tell her?

'Dance school. He was gentle, danced beautifully and was very sexy, which he apparently didn't realise. I think that's what made him attractive; he didn't swagger his good looks. There was something chemical about him, pheromones I guess, made me want to shag him if I stood within a couple of feet.'

'And you fell in love.'

'I seduced him. Honestly, that's the word to use as he had to be persuaded. I was living with someone else and he didn't think it was right.' Pausing to run his tongue over his lips, he screwed up his face with concentration. 'He could read my mind.'

She frowned.

'We were lying in bed one afternoon, and he was dozing. I was reading a comic book and he suddenly woke up. He told me the dream he'd had and it was an exact match for the comic I was holding. He hadn't seen it. Have you ever been that close to someone?'

She smiled. 'I've heard stories. How did your affair end?'

'He called me to say it was all or nothing. Either we were going to be together properly or not at all. It was only three weeks, I wasn't sure what I really felt for him and he was so impatient, he just didn't understand I needed more time to sort things out. He wanted everything to be perfect, which was just so bloody unrealistic! Oooh. My head's spinning. What did you say your name was again?'

'Elspet, I'm called Elspet.'

'Can I have a glass of water, Elspet? By the way, I think your cats are eating my puke.'

'They do that, they like tidying up. But you haven't finished your story. What happened to bring you back together?'

'Dance school reunion. I wanted to see him again. We both brought our other halves, his wife Nathalie and my husband Brian. I felt sorry for them as the rest of us were being luvvies all night, as we caught up with people. There was a moment, when Greg and I sat together at a crowded table. I leaned my leg against his and he squeezed my hand under the table. We've been shagging since then. This is our first weekend away together. I'm sorry, it's getting hard to concentrate. I could really do with that water. By the way, has anyone ever told you what a beautiful young woman you are? I thought you were older, but how old are you? Twenty?'

'Something like that. I'll get your water. Rest peacefully.'

She rose and tightened her tweed skirt at the sides before leaving the room.

As she entered the mementoes room, Gregory rose from the chair.

'How is he?'

'Resting. You're staring again.'

'I'm sorry, it's just that I thought you were … different. Is your name Elspet?'

'That's right. You can go in and see your friend if you wish. He asked for a glass of water. I'll fetch it for you.'

Gregory followed her into the kitchen and took the glass of water she got from the tap. He decided he must have hit his head when the car crashed into the tree, as he could have sworn she looked older when they first met. She led the way back to the bedroom, then left him to enter by himself.

Inside, he had to shake Alex's shoulder to wake him.

'Here, you should drink this.'

Alex blinked and looked confused.

'Where am I?' He focussed on Gregory. 'Who are you? Where's Brian?'

'Alex, it's me, Gregory.'

'I don't know you, get away from me. I want Brian, he's my husband, I want Brian!'

Alex sat up in bed. Gregory took his hand and held it, and soothingly stroked his forehead with the other.

'Ssh, ssh. Don't be scared.'

Alex was sweating, but his skin felt cold to Gregory.

He took deep breaths as if he was struggling to find air, and gulped like a drowning man. Gregory looked into his eyes and saw the pupils quickly dilate as his body juddered and then stopped moving.

'I love you,' Gregory whispered.

He laid Alex on the bed and wiped tears and snot from his own face.

The cats leapt from the floor onto Alex and licked the salt sweat from his face and hands.

'Get off! Leave him!'

They didn't move and so he picked up two of them, regardless of claws and teeth, and threw them as gently as he could into the hall, not wanting to harm them. It was close; he wanted to throw them against the wall and see them splatter like bladders of skin and bone. The third took the cue and fled.

Gregory leant against the door frame, sobbing. It took him a couple of minutes to recover, before he shuffled back to the memento room in search of the woman.

She was sitting in the arm chair, with her ankles crossed, stroking one of the cats which sat on her lap. Another sat on the table beside her and the third perched on the chair back, beside her head. All eyes swung to him as he entered.

'You'd better sit down. I'm sorry about your friend. I think he had a ruptured spleen. You could have saved him, if you got help to him immediately.'

'I tried, you said you'd called the police, the ambulance.'

'I told you there was no phone here. But we could have driven him to the hospital, if you'd asked me, but you said he was already dead.'

He sat in the chair beside her.

'Why are you lying?'

'Just rehearsing my story, for the police. They'll be here soon.'

She indicated the patio doors. Gregory saw the flashing blue lights near the remaining glow from the burning car. He turned his head back and looked more closely at the shelves. Amongst the modern objects he'd recognised earlier, there were older items: Victorian pocket watches, ladies fans and hair pieces, playing cards, chess pieces, wooden bowls and bronze axes.

'Who are you?'

'One who loves stories.'

'You live off them?'

She smiled her agreement. 'You know of story tellers, I am a story *taker*. As you've seen, they keep me young. He didn't recognise you, did he, wanted his husband, Brian?'

'He was dying, confused.'

'He'd forgotten you. In telling me the story of his love for you, he fed me his memories. Considering the disappointment you were to him, I think I did him a kindness.'

'That's monstrous.'

She laughed and then stood. As she talked, she moved to kneel at the side of his chair and took hold of his hand.

'You people drink to forget, take drugs to escape the horror of remembrance. You eliminate not only the pain, but your joy, love of children, memories of families, hopes and desires. I take only what you tell me, only what you wish to loose. I am more subtle than a surgeon's probe, burning the flesh of the brain to remove the nightmares.'

Stroking the side of his face, she said. 'I am more gentle than a husband's betrayal; which scalds a wife's memories of love and excites fear and hatred in their children. I am more kind than a bullet through your temple, as the final attempt to shatter the roiling clouds of guilt, shame and pleasure which addle you. All your shame and guilt at your cowardice will be gone with no chance of reminder; as there will be no memories to stir, no images, no scents and no words, to wake desire for his caresses. You will be free of him. All you need do is tell me your story and give me a memento.'

She stood and walked to the window and watched the police lights.

'You don't have much time to make your decision.' She looked at him quickly. 'Unless, of course, you prefer to tell me all about Nathalie and your children, so you can remember your first and truest love?' Giggling quietly, she returned to her wing back chair. 'That would be funny.'

After a few moments, he pulled the photo of him and Alex from his jacket and handed it to her.

'I was a virgin when we met, away from home. We were all teenagers, searching for the truth of ourselves, celebrating our discoveries with our bodies. There was a party; he spoke with me for hours. Something in me danced at his touch. I don't mean the sex. I mean … I thought I'd crippled it when we split up.

'Anyway, at the reunion I held his hand and felt it again. You can call it "just pheromones", but that doesn't make it unreal or without joy. It was good. We were good together.'

He told her everything he could remember; the stolen moments between classes, the jokes, the texture of Alex's skin, the sound of his voice; all the minutiae of their time at school and their meetings since the reunion.

She insisted he tell everything they'd done since he'd met Alex at the train station that morning. It was important that when the police questioned him, he appear the victim of amnesia.

At the end, she leant over him and kissed him full on the mouth. He was so surprised, he hardly responded, except to notice the coldness of her tongue, as it probed his mouth.

'Ah, strawberry jam,' she said.

He walked away from the house, oblivious to the sound of cat's jaws crunching Alex's bones. Happy he could no longer remember he was once, inconveniently, loved. Happy, as he'd forgotten he no longer loved his wife.

His mouth tasted of dust.

SPOILERS

Through my open car window, I said my name into the intercom and the tall, wrought iron gates swung open.

It took nearly a minute to reach the top of the gravel drive to the mansion, through woodland which the headlights hardly penetrated.

I stopped the car and looked at the house. Only the portico and the large living room on the ground floor were lit—the latter by just a couple of table lamps. He wanted to keep things intimate.

As I got out of the car, he pulled open the front door and stepped back to allow me to enter. I admired his taste in clothes; the way his shirt hung softly showed its expense and he'd spent money on his face, the skin was too unwrinkled for his age. I assumed his physique came from hours in his home gym and he was a strong as he looked. I'd have to be careful.

He appraised me as I entered, like an owner studying a thoroughbred. I was twenty-eight and he liked the look of me.

'Through there,' he said, indicating the living room. 'Take a seat. Do you want a drink, before we …'

'You'll die soon,' I said.

He looked puzzled. 'What? What did you say?'

'Shall I tell you when?'

'What are you talking about?'

'Your timely, unnatural and really quite hideous death. Thought you might like to know when it will happen.'

'Look, if this is part of the role play, or a joke, it's not funny. I haven't hired you to play silly buggers.'

'No. No joke.'

'Get out or I'll call the police.'

'You'll find the phone's not working. Temporary fault, which will resolve itself after I leave.'

He picked up the phone and listened to silence for a few moments, then started looking round the room.

'Mobile's not working either. Family are out. Your staff have a night off.'

He went to a desk and pulled open the right hand drawer, keeping an eye on me. The drawer was empty.

'It's here,' I said, holding up the small revolver I'd taken earlier in the day.

'Who are you?'

'Someone who knows a lot about you, including the aforementioned place, time and manner of your death. Not tonight you understand. But soon. You might as well sit. You might also want to pour yourself that drink.'

Slightly confused by the order of my instructions, it took him a moment to work out he needed to get the drink first, and then sit.

'Are you sitting comfortably?' I said. 'Then I'll begin. Before we go further, are you more concerned by the "When?", or the "How?".'

He looked at the ice in his drink. Then around the room, I assume looking for a route of escape, or another way to summon help. He eyed the metal poker next to the log fire.

'Please,' I said, pointing the gun more directly at him. 'I'll have taken out a knee before you've stood.'

More staring at the ice in his drink.

'When?'

'It will be soon. Certainly in the foreseeable future. I appreciate that's a very inexact unit to measure time.'

'Why are you telling me this?'

'Interesting question. Not, "Why is this happening?". I detect a note of guilt. You've been expecting something. The other question, you might reasonably ask is "Where?".

'It wouldn't work,' he said. 'If I knew where, I wouldn't go there. Therefore, you won't tell me, or you'll lie.'

'Well done! You got there remarkably quickly. We all have our own appointment in Samarkand, Samarra—or wherever. It might be poetic if we took you to the cave on the estate, where you like to play. You've proved no-one can hear screams from there.'

He shuddered.

'After I've gone, and you consider your options, don't think you can play hide and seek with us. We haven't travelled off planet yet, but I'm sure we would if necessary.'

'Us? Who the hell are you?'

I smiled. 'We have many names.'

'You're not actually going to tell me anything useful, are you?'

I considered this. 'I might.'

I walked to a window, turning my back to him. It made me vulnerable to attack, but I don't think he noticed, and I could see his reflection. It's always a good test to see how much trouble we might have later on.

I checked my watch. We still had fifteen minutes before the phones came back. I should really have left then, but I wanted, needed, another drink and I wanted to play.

'So,' I said. 'Shall we talk about the weather? We're British, so I think we should. I can tell you, with confidence, your death will not be weather related. Especially in the sense of: you deciding to favour ruby slippers and a tornado dumping a house on you. I do hope that's some kind of comfort. Not having a house drop on you, whilst wearing ruby slippers. I mean to say, how embarrassing would that be? Can't you just imagine the press and the headlines: "Thirty-eight year old man found wearing ruby slippers, crushed by ..." Wait a minute, you're thirty-six now, aren't you?'

'Yes,' he said.

'I'm sorry. You must have heard "thirty-eight", and thought, "Hey, I've got at least a couple of years. Lots of people get told six months. Two years, that's not so bad. Time to get things sorted. Time to knock a few more things off the bucket list." Didn't you? Sorry. No. Slip of the tongue. Definitely will not be weather related. It will be human hands. With, perhaps, machines. Or, what we like to refer to as: "the tools of the trade." Our little joke.'

He started shivering, and his head dropped forward.

'Oh, do stop crying, or I'll give you something to cry about!'

He looked up at me.

'Why do parents say that to children?' I said. 'Really, why do they think threatening a child with violence will induce them not to cry? Fear, I suppose. They expect to frighten their child into being quiet. So many people use fear to control others. World religions; governments terrorise us with terrorists so they can take away our liberties; large corporations; they sew our lives with threads of fear, so they can pull on them like puppeteers and we dance to their tune. Control freaks.'

I strode over to him and slapped his face with the gun.

'You liked controlling them, didn't you? Those boys. Didn't you?'

He lay back on the sofa, protecting his face with his hands.

'I'm sorry! I'm sorry.'

'Stop grizzling! Saying sorry now won't make any difference.'

I went to the bar and poured a drink, watching him in the mirror which hung above it.

'Do you know how long I've had to do this job? How often I've had to talk to bastards like you?'

'Of course I bloody don't!'

I turned to face him.

'I'm sorry,' I said. 'That was unprofessional. This is supposed to be about you. I'm supposed to be warning you. Letting you know that we know, and that some of us will visit you again.'

He looked up at me and then spat. It was childish. He immediately raised his arms to protect his face, as if I was about to strike him again. I didn't. I wiped his spittle from my face.

'Where was I? … Right, yes, bucket list. Strange really how so many people's bucket lists include activities likely to result in death. Perverse, to feel you have to be close to death in order to feel alive. Daring Death.'

I felt tired and took a seat opposite him. He moved back in his seat, to get away from me. I leaned back and lifted my leg over one of the arms, letting the gun rest on my crotch.

'I wonder about the poor buggers who do have a list and don't complete it,' I said. 'I think it's very sad that if all they're saying of you at your funeral is: "He didn't complete his list, you know? He had another four to go."'

'Are you ever going to shut up?' he said.

'Not long now. Soon be over. That's what they say in hospital, isn't it? When they're doing something particularly unpleasant and painful to you, to help you get through the suffering. They want you to focus on the time when you won't be in pain.'

I smiled at him.

'Perhaps you could do that. Wake up each morning and say to yourself, "Not long now, soon be over." Because, well I mean, it's going to be true for you, isn't it? You're going to be released from this vale of tears. *Released* is probably the wrong word. Released implies setting free and then enjoying your freedom. I don't know and really can't speculate on what's coming next for you; after we've finished with you, I mean. Have to say, purely personally and not making representations on behalf of my employers; that I really hope it will not be pleasant. We both know that you do not deserve heaven over hell. I've seen the pictures.'

'I ... I ... I can't help it.'

I laughed loudly, slapping my knee.

'Thanks. You've just won me a tenner. I have a standing bet with some of the lads, that I'll hear that line when I visit.'

I got up and poured myself a drink. I looked at him and asked him if he wanted another, by waggling the bottle and indicating he should come over. He picked up his glass and walked cautiously to me. I smiled and he relaxed slightly. As he came close, I punched him hard in the stomach, then on the jaw.

'Sorry, I couldn't help myself.'

He staggered to a nearby chair and sat.

'It does amaze me how many people believe they're going to heaven, in spite of – and in some cases, because of – the way they've persecuted, maimed or promulgated hatred for their fellow man, woman and child. I don't think you'd put yourself in that category would you? You don't consider yourself a man with a cause or a god on your side. I know you consider yourself as beyond the law. To an extent you're right. You're certainly beyond the reach of the courts of the land. That's why I'm here. To let you know that justice will still be done.'

I picked up my coat from the back of a chair and looked at him whilst I pulled it on.

'Word of advice. When they do come for you, they are not in a position to negotiate. Seriously, you'd be surprised at the number of people who try to persuade, cajole and bribe their way out. Actually, you could try bribing them. The lads like that. You see, they listen very carefully to your proposition and then they discuss it. Well, they usually just mutter "rhubarb, rhubarb" and try not to laugh too loudly. So, they don't discuss it, take the money and finish the job anyway. All you've achieved is giving yourself a bit of hope, a bit more time perhaps, but really all you've done is prolong your own suffering. You can see why we laugh about it.'

I stood in front of him, with my hands in the pockets of the coat.

'You know what's really funny? You're going to try it anyway. You will, you know. It's human nature. You'll beg, plead, curse, bribe. I'm telling you it will be no good and you will do it anyway. Some don't. But I think you will. You look the grovelling kind.'

I pulled on my gloves and tied my scarf.

'Right, I really must be going, I have others on my list for tonight.'

As I got to the door, I turned: I've always loved Columbo.

'Just one more thing. You know, there was one chap who changed after our little chat. I still grin when I think about him. You see, it suddenly dawned on him that he had time – a little time, like you – to really think about why I was talking to him. He decided to do better. He did his utmost to repair what he'd done wrong. Couldn't of course, couldn't change anything. Not rich like you, but he tried to make amends. When we came to do our job, well, he wasn't exactly happy; but he was satisfied. Truly inspirational.'

'What can I do? To escape this.'

I sighed. 'You're really not listening are you? I'm beginning to think you'll put this down to a bad trip.'

I shot him in the foot and waited for him to stop screaming.

'This really is happening and you really do have to understand. The game is up and we really are going to hurt you, very much. If you decide to go on a final spree, before we come for you, then this will happen: we will come earlier, take you to a very dark, quiet place and make sure you stay alive until the originally agreed time. We'll use you for training purpose, let the interns "have a go". Does them so much good, the interns that is. Same amount of time, just more suffering.'

I took a napkin from the bar. 'Here, you can use this to stop the blood. Just tell the ambulance people you had an accident with the gun. Bloody silly of you.'

I emptied the gun of the remaining bullets and placed it on the bar.

'Now, I must be going. You really mustn't worry about all this, you know. There's no point. You can't run, can't hide. I mean, you can try, but we're like the Canadian Mounties, we always get our man. Or woman and very occasionally, sadly, a child. So no need to worry, as there is absolutely nothing you can do. Worrying will not make a difference to the final outcome.

'As I said, you will hear from us again. I'll let myself out.'

As I left the room, I heard him slump to the floor, but I didn't look back.

I wish I was a psychopath, didn't feel things. But I do and that's why I bloody hate my job.

Perhaps I've just been doing it for too long. It was different when I started. Then, there was a real sense of job satisfaction; that we do what we do to the deserving, to balance the scales of justice.

Recently, things have changed here.

You know, I used to tell the deserving … that's what we call them, by the way. Those who we visit. It's like any club, we have our jargon.

The deserving, those who we visit and upon whom we *visit justice*: that is rip, torture, maim and finally kill.

I'm a *visitor*, though herald might be a better word. I let the deserving know what's coming to them. We do it, I think from a sense of tradition, as it would be a damn sight simpler for *the deliverers* to just turn up and deliver justice unannounced. It would be easier for all of us; as half the time the deserving run away and we have to go to the bother of following them. We don't have to find them—as we never lose anyone.

You see, we're a very ancient organisation, founded to carry out the work of the original Star Chamber. It was a group set up by the king to deal with the powerful; those who might be beyond the law due to their riches or position at court. As the trials were held in secret and many were condemned in absentia they needed to be visited. The visitation was a chance for them to put their affairs in order and to do "the honourable thing".

I think a few did kill themselves. Long ago.

Certainly, I can think of only one person who's taken that option since I've been here. He was a coward. Just couldn't face what he thought was coming to him. I may have made sure he'd understood that we'd visit justice on him in terms of a blow by blow, wound by wound, pain by pain, recreation of what he'd done to his victims. Possibly, that we'd do that more than once. Which was unprofessional of me, but I'd read his file.

That's another old fashioned thing about us, everything is either typed on a manual typewriter or hand written. Seriously, it's 2014 and we commit records only to paper. It's far more secure than using computers.

Here's how it works. We have *witnesses* everywhere. Banks, hospitals, police stations, newspapers and television and it's their job to inform the *recording angels* of one of the deserving. The recording angel collates all documentation, transcribes any videos, and places the papers into a brown manila file.

The file is then reviewed by the *privy councillors*. Not the ones you might see on TV, but the real privy councillors. On the inside front cover of the file, an ink line is drawn down the centre. After reviewing the paperwork, each privy councillor puts a tick to either left or right of that line. No signatures or initials, just a tick. If all seven are to the left of the line, the file comes to one of us visitors. If there is a dissenting mark, then a horizontal line is drawn across the inside cover and the process is repeated until all seven agree. Very occasionally, they might meet in the board room to discuss a case. More often than not, I suspect the sight of a lone tick to the right of the line is enough to convince that councillor to follow the others. I've never seen a file which has gone round three times.

When we visitors receive the file, the first page is always a sheet of paper with a typed name and address. No letterhead, no company name, nothing. It's the only piece of paper which leaves this building.

We have an hour with the file to review it, so we understand the crimes. Then we make our visit and add a single page of notes to the file, which is then passed to deliverers, via the recording angels. When the deliverers receive the file, there is a new piece of paper, with the name, address and a date. Visitors aren't told the date beforehand, but we're usually told when the job is finished. So, yes, I lied when I said I knew when he'd die.

When the deliverers are finished, they add another page to the file. The file is then passed back to a recording angel, who checks that justice has indeed been visited on the deserving. The file is burned. There's no point in keeping it as there can be no appeal.

When I started, I thought our logo could be justice, with her blindfold removed and her sword raised. Now I think it should just be a fat arse shitting in her scales. Something has changed.

This morning, Lord Haining called me into his office.

'How are you doing Peter?' he said.

'I'm fine sir.'

'Only, I heard you visited the room the other day.'

'Yes, sir. It was after the Hilliam visitation of justice sir. The deliverers were short staffed and I was asked to assist. It's been a long time since I was a deliverer sir and well, you read the file. What he did. What we … did. Well … you read the file.'

'Yes, yes, I see. Quite understandable.'

I should tell you about *the room*. It's very ordinary and usually it's kept locked. Anyone can ask for the key. It's all part of the retirement plan. You have two choices. One, you retire to a nice walled and heavily guarded estate, in Yorkshire. Two, you ask for the key to the room.

When you enter the room, you'll find a chair and a table. The walls, floors and ceilings are all tiled white. There is a drain in the corner of the room and a tap, with a hose attached, in the opposite corner. On the table, if you're a woman, there will be a glass of a colourless liquid, smelling slightly of burnt almonds. If you're a man there's a revolver with one bullet. As I said; we are very traditional.

The door to the room is always locked behind you and someone watches you on closed circuit TV. You can stay in there as long as you like. You can also knock on the door and ask to be let out. But you'd better be quick. One of the recording angels, a man, sat in there once, simply crying for nearly three hours. The deliverers entered and did the job for him. Someone obviously thought it was the kindest thing. Or perhaps they got bored of watching him.

'This file is different,' said Lord Haining.

He handed me a file and I opened it. There were only five ticks to the left of the line. The rest of the cover was blank.

'I'm sorry sir, I don't understand.'

'There's been a change in policy; five is now all that is necessary. There have been funding cuts.'

I started flipping through the pages, expecting to see the usual stomach churning photos, but there weren't any. All I could find were phone conversations, notes on his YouTube videos. I recognised him. He was popular for his rage against bankers.

'But sir, this isn't our sort of work.'

'Strickland, how long have you worked here?'

'That's my personnel file on your desk, sir. You can look it up.'

'I can also look up the names of your loved ones, can't I? Please don't make me do it.'

I became very aware of my own breathing.

Loved ones are a key staff motivator. They're also a liability. Ellinson was another visitor. His family died in fog, in a motorway pile up. After the funeral, he was in the office one day. The next, I was given his workload. I never knew if he'd visited the room or gone to Yorkshire.

Killing your boss has to be considered a career terminating move, but the bastard was threatening my wife and daughter, to force me to do a political job.

As I said, I used to be a deliverer. Before that, I was a member of the UK Special Forces. I was recruited here after I was paroled from my sentence for manslaughter. He was my best friend. We were drunk. He'd jumped out at me, from a bush on a dark, frosty moonless night. He grabbed me round the neck, his forearm across my throat, tousling my hair, laughing at me. We were drunk. He wasn't army, he didn't know. My training reacted, not me.

Before Lord Haining could drop to the floor, I caught him and sat him in his chair. I swung it so it was facing the window – which had blinds – away from the door. I placed my personnel file within the one he'd shown me and headed to the door.

As I opened it, I turned to look back into the room. I raised my voice slightly and said: 'Yes, Lord Haining, I'll tell her. You're not to be disturbed for an hour.'

I closed the door behind me and looked at Helen, Lord Haining's assistant. 'You heard, did you?'

'Yes, but he's only getting half an hour. He's due with the others for a conference call with the USA. I'd better remind him.' She stood to walk to the door. For a moment I thought I'd have to kill her too.

The phone rang on her desk.

'Helen, you take that. I'll nip back in and tell him.'

'Thanks, Mr Strickland.'

I walked back into the office, closed the door behind me and walked to Haining's desk, told his corpse he had half an hour, waited long enough for a grunted reply and left.

Helen was still on the phone, explaining that Lord Haining wasn't taking any calls and they'd have to call back. Knowing Helen, unless it was God on the phone, the call wouldn't be put through. I smiled at her as I left.

I waited in the corridor outside her office, apparently reading the files, but also waiting to confirm she'd put off the call. It took a couple of minutes, but she did. That meant I probably had only twenty or so minutes left, as she was bound to remind Haining at least five minutes before the USA call was due.

Waiting outside the office, I had time to look at my personnel file. Clipped to the front were two pieces of paper. The first had my name and address on it. The second, that of my wife Jenna and daughter Cherise. I wasn't sure if Haining had meant to use those pieces of paper as leverage, to show he meant business; or he'd meant to use them anyway.

I headed for the basement, where all completed files were burned. I stopped in the corridor to give myself time to think, and looked up at the security cameras. Apart from the offices of the privy councillors, the damn things are everywhere.

It's a very simple system. The camera monitors are watched 24 hours. To keep guards awake, they have to produce handwritten reports on everyone in the building. Every fifteen minutes, a note is made of what each of us is doing. Those notes are reviewed by recording angels and, if any suspicious behaviour is noticed, it's referred to the privy councillors.

I flicked through the rest of my personnel file. Nothing. No notes reporting suspicious behaviour. Good. I looked at the camera and waved. I then mimed that I was coming to see them.

I knocked on their door and waited for it to be unlocked.

Albert peered round the door.

'Is there a problem, sir?' he said.

'Nothing for you to worry about, but I need to observe one of the angels.'

He let me in the room. I entered and he locked the door behind me. His colleague, Meredith, was busy writing a note about someone on a screen and had her back to us. I let Albert walk towards his desk, then stepped behind him and broke his neck.

'Albert, what's wrong?' I said, as he fell. 'Meredith, come give me a hand.'

She turned in her chair, then knelt and slapped Albert's face a few times. I stepped back to give her room.

I hesitated. I liked Meredith.

I thought of Jenna and Cherise, and as Meredith looked up at me I used the heel of my hand to force the bone in her nose up into her brain. I wiped my eyes free of tears and felt the cold sweat trickle down my back.

I watched the monitors for a few minutes, to ensure I could leave the room without being seen in the corridor. I left the room, locking it behind me, and walked to the basement.

Derek was sitting at the front desk, eating a sandwich, with a pile of four files beside him.

'Hi Derek,' I said.

'Oh, hello Mr Strickland. What brings you down here?'

'Special request from Lord Haining. He wants this completed file destroyed now.'

'Well, add it to the pile and I'll get round to it after I've finished my sandwich.'

'I think he really meant now, as in tout de suite.'

He eyed me suspiciously. 'Well, this is most irregular. Not sure about this.' He reached for the phone, but stopped half way, suddenly realising, I think, that he wasn't sure who to call. He certainly wasn't about to call Lord Haining and I suspected he didn't want to mess with Helen either.

I'd never really got to know Derek and his unhelpful attitude was earning him a death sentence. As I stepped forward to remove his doubts, permanently, I heard the door open behind me.

It was Grossmith, a deliverer.

'Oh, hello Mr Grossmith, perhaps you can help us, I was just explaining to Mr Strickland here – Jeesus! What are you doing?' said Derek.

'What do you mean?' I said. 'You just watched me take a pen from my pocket and shove it in Mr Grossmith's eye.'

Grossmith was still standing, twitching as if he was being electrocuted. He also gurgled. I nudged him and he toppled backwards, falling against the door, closing and blocking it.

'Right,' I said. 'Are you going to let me burn these files, Derek?'

'Yuh, yes.' He said, standing and swaying slightly.

'OK. Show me the way and we'll do this together.'

Derek stood and led me behind the desk to the incinerator. He opened the door and I felt the heat from the gas jets. I guess he kept them lit all the time.

There was a conveyor system leading inside the incinerator and Derek placed the files on it. I watched as they moved into the heart of the machine and burn.

Derek looked at me, sweating and scared.

'Please, Mr Strickland. I have a wife and three kids. Bethany's only—'

'I have a family too,' I said.

I left his body where it fell. I needed time to think, but knew I didn't have any.

'Fuck' I said, as I rolled Grossmith's body away from the door. 'Four down ... gods dammit, I mean five down.' Ten minutes and I'd already lost count. How many more to go? I couldn't see myself successfully murdering the entire staff by hand. I really didn't want to.

'Fuck, fuck—'

I shut my mouth, tight, to stop the sound of my voice and paced the room and looking for inspiration.

'Oh, you beauty,' I said, as I spotted the red fire alarm button. I used my elbow to smash it.

The bell was bloody loud, particularly in the confines of the basement.

I ran up the stairs and found a young angel carrying a file a few steps from the top, heading down.

'What are you gawping at you idiot? This isn't a drill, get the hell out.' He dropped the file and fled.

I went back to my desk, picked up my fire warden's arm band and headed for Lord Haining's office. I shouted at people not to run, but walk, as I hurried past them.

I met Helen coming towards me.

'Has Lord Haining come out of his office?' I said.

She looked slightly guilty.

'I didn't check,' she said.

'Good girl,' I said, smiling cheerfully at her. 'You did the right thing. You run along, it's my job to check everyone's out.'

She hurried off, her heels clacking on the polished wooden floor.

Inside Haining's office, I found his drinks cabinet and the bottle of brandy I knew he kept there. It was more than three quarters full.

I opened it and doused my hanky in some of the brandy and then shoved it well into the bottle, leaving a couple of inches protruding from the neck. It took me a few moments to find Haining's lighter in his left trouser pocket.

There was no point going to the file room. They'd designed metal, fireproof doors to protect the files. A senior recording angel would have ensured all files were placed in it before locking it and leaving the building.

I had a key to the stationery room. That was full of paper. Lots of paper as we ran the entire organisation on pieces of the stuff. That and the small bottles of highly flammable white liquid we used to correct our typing mistakes.

It was very satisfying to hurl the flaming Molotov cocktail into the room.

As I said, we were an ancient and traditional organisation, which meant many of the walls were still oak panelled. They were centuries old and dry.

I stood with the others outside as I watched the building go up in flames wonderfully quickly.

As the fire brigade arrived, I slipped away, to see Jenna and Cherise. The restraining order Jenna took out against me soon after I'd come out of prison meant I couldn't speak to them. That didn't mean I couldn't watch unobserved as Jenna picked Cherise up from school. It doesn't mean I don't love them.

Emptying my bank accounts was done within an hour of the fire brigade arriving. I booked into a quiet boarding house in Brighton to work out what to do next.

Dazed, I was finding it hard to think clearly. On the drive from London I stopped at services on the M23. I thought I recognised some of the other people in the cafe. They looked like people I'd met as either visitor or deliverer. My mind was playing tricks on me, which was frightening.

In my bedroom in Brighton, with its candlewick bedspread over sheets and blankets, I sat with a notebook, writing out my plans. There was no need to travel to Yorkshire, to destroy the retirement home. I'd worked out years ago; it was a complete fiction. There had only ever been the room, or natural death, as an exit policy.

The original Star Chamber was disbanded after it simply became a way to remove political enemies. I decided to visit justice upon the remaining members of the real privy council. Then I realised I didn't know who they were. I cried then. Tears of loss, anger and frustration choked me. I thought of Helen, she would know. I would visit her.

I contemplated what I'd done, what I was about to do. I tried thinking of myself as some sort of avenging hero, a man with a just and righteous cause. It didn't work. I'd met too many of them. Looked into too many eyes and seen the self-delusion; the greed, the anger or fear which really drove them.

I see my eyes in the bathroom mirror.

I am no psychopath; I liked the people I killed.

THIS TOO SOLID FLESH

Caroline was disappointed in the nice young man guiding the tour of the poison garden. She'd paid for her ticket to learn which plants were the most poisonous, which would cause the nastiest death. He told the group how few plant poisonings there were each year, as the poisons tasted so bitter. He also pointed out they'd all be found in an autopsy.

She felt cheated.

Caroline left the garden at the end of the tour and bought a book on poisonous plants at the garden's gift shop. Surely there was some plant she could use? The garden didn't have *every* poisonous plant. She was about to use her debit card to pay for the book, but hesitated, and paid cash.

Tanya was drinking cappuccino in the café, flipping through a glossy fashion magazine. Caroline sat at the table, opposite her best friend.

'Sorry I was late for the tour,' said Tanya. 'They said I couldn't go in once it had started, so I came here to wait for you. I thought you'd find me.'

'Don't worry,' said Caroline. 'It's not as if you've never been late before.'

Tanya laughed an acknowledgement and took a sip of coffee, missing the flash of anger in Caroline's eyes. Tanya's lateness for any appointment with Caroline started when they became friends at school, and continued throughout their time at university. If Tanya was late for everything, then it wouldn't have mattered so much; but she was punctual for work and other friends never complained. Over the years, each minute past every appointment dripped resentment into Caroline's anger. She'd passed the red, flaming stage years ago and now the anger curdled in her stomach, grey and warm. All Caroline wanted was for the gnawing in her belly to stop.

'What are you smiling about?' asked Tanya.

'Oh, nothing. Something silly.'

Tanya frowned, and returned to her magazine.

Caroline bit her lower lip to suppress her smile at the thought of "the late Tanya".

In her hotel room that evening, the book on poison plants proved as frustrating as the tour, as it reiterated modern forensics would quickly identify the cause of death. The only way she'd avoid prison was if no-one thought Tanya's death was malicious. Caroline packed the book deep in her suitcase and decided to only read it alone.

They returned from their holiday in Northumbria, to their home in Trafalgar Road, Horsham on Saturday afternoon.

In bed, Caroline read more of the book and decided she didn't have to kill Tanya. Making her ill would be more satisfying.

Her parents probably had what she needed, and after Sunday lunch she rummaged in their garden shed.

At work on Monday, Caroline received an email from Tanya at ten o'clock.

'See you for lunch today, at 1pm in the café above the bookshop in the Carfax. T.'

No question mark, this was a bloody command, not an invitation. And she knew where the bookshop was; there was only one in town which had a café. Her stomach knotted.

Caroline wanted to be late arriving, but she worked in the internal service desk; so her lunch was literally an hour. Tanya worked three floors above her in the insurance company as an executive in the marketing department. Her lunch hours were more flexible.

Caroline looked out the window of the bookshop's first floor café. She thought of the daffodil bulbs she'd taken from her parents, sitting next to the onions in the larder at home, and wondered if she could hand Tanya a salad made with them without her hand shaking. They wouldn't kill her, but she'd be vomiting for a couple of days.

As the minute hand on Caroline's watch touched twenty past one, her jaw clenched shut and she rehearsed in her mind cutting the bulbs, decided how to mix them with the onions and lettuce, what dressing to use and how she'd make sure she didn't eat any. Or perhaps it would be better if she did, so Tanya wouldn't suspect her.

Tanya walked quickly along the road outside the bookshop. She looked up from her phone and waved at Caroline, who bit her lower lip; worried her thoughts of poison might show in her face.

As Tanya climbed the stairs inside the bookshop to the café, she continued her phone conversation and only ended it when she reached the counter to order her lunch. Other diners, who were mostly elderly, scowled at her.

Tanya sat opposite Caroline, removed her expensive silk scarf and placed it in her handbag.

'Sorry I'm late,' said Tanya. 'Meeting over-ran. I hope they bring my salad quickly. I've got another one at two-thirty and I need to prepare. You look well.'

'Do I? I don't feel it.'

'Ooh. Before I forget, I must tell you my news; my promotion interview is on Thursday, so wish me luck.'

Caroline's stomach rumbled.

'I thought the job was more or less yours anyway.'

'Well, yes. But there are other candidates, including three external applicants. That's the trouble with the collapse of the banking sector. There are a lot of good people around.'

Tanya checked her watch and looked towards the kitchen. A tall waiter with curly brown hair and short beard approached their table, carrying two plates of food. Caroline saw him too, and blushed. He had such lovely brown eyes and she felt ashamed she fancied him.

'Ah, Marco, thank you,' said Tanya. 'Mine's the chicken salad.'

'And the cheese baguette is for you, signorina,' said Marco. 'Should I bring your cake now or later?'

Caroline's blush deepened as Tanya raised an eyebrow at the word "cake", and she became conscious of how tightly her clothes fitted.

'Later will be fine.'

Tanya unashamedly watched Marco's tight rear as he walked back to the kitchen. She shivered with delight. 'I wonder if he's available.'

'I thought you were seeing Jimmy.'

'I am … well, in his mind anyway.'

'He always asks after you.'

'I mean he's good as a regular fuck,' said Tanya. 'But, honestly, he's getting a bit too intense. Why do some men want to tie you down, get married, have kids?'

'I honestly have no idea.'

'I'll probably dump him on Friday, so he can get over me at the weekend. Besides, if I get the job, I'll be based in London. I'll commute at first, but I'll look for somewhere to live up there.'

Tanya continued eating, but Caroline put the baguette down so she could process the information. Tanya leaving meant finding a new housemate or moving back with her parents. She couldn't think of anything to say.

At the next table, Marco brought a woman a mushroom omelette, and Caroline had a new idea.

After lunch, Caroline was hanging her coat in the office when Jimmy walked up to her.

'How's Tanya?' he said.

She liked his Welsh accent.

'She's fine. And, no, she didn't mention you … though I'm sure she meant to send her love. She had a meeting to get to.'

Oh, shit. Why had she said that? She'd just thrown him a crumb of hope, and that was cruel. But it was hard not to please him. He was a couple of years younger than she and Tanya, and had recently finished his time on the graduate programme. He had a "lost puppy" look about him, despite being tall and a rugby player.

As Jimmy walked away he checked his mobile phone. Caroline assumed he was looking for a message from Tanya. He started a new text, but abandoned it as he sat at his desk.

Caroline followed him.

'Look, Jimmy. About Tanya …'

He looked up at her, but the phone on the desk rang. He smiled apologetically at her, put on his headset and said: 'Service Desk. Jimmy speaking, how can I help?'

He didn't look at her as he typed details of the call into the help-desk software.

Caroline sighed and went to her desk.

That evening, Caroline was reaching for a daffodil bulb to add to the salad, when Tanya spoke:

'I'm sorry about earlier.'

Caroline's hand rested on the bulb and she looked at her.

'I'm sorry, what?'

'Telling you I might be moving out like that, I didn't mean to be so insensitive. I was so caught up in the prospect of the promotion, I didn't think about how it would affect you. I mean getting a new housemate and everything.'

Caroline picked up an onion and diced it. The blade moved rapidly and she imagined finishing the onion, turning and slitting Tanya's throat. She closed her eyes.

'It's O.K., it's important to you.'

'Thanks, Caroline. I knew you'd understand and I will help you look for a new housemate. And it's not like we'll never see each other again. You can help me look for a flat.'

There it is, Caroline thought. *She means I can do the donkey work. She doesn't deserve this promotion, doesn't deserve to live a glamorous lifestyle in London, not after what she's going to do to Jimmy.*

'Are you listening?' said Tanya. 'I said, you'll be able to come up at weekends and we can enjoy the sights and nightclubs.'

'Yes. Yes, of course. Lay the table please. I'll dish up.'

The daffodil bulbs were untouched. If she gave them to Tanya on Wednesday, then she'd be vomiting on Thursday, and she'd miss the interview and she wouldn't move out.

After dinner they watched a movie, curled on the sofa.

Tanya's mobile rang. She checked the caller ID, smiled, found the remote control and silenced the TV.

She twirled her blonde hair round her free index finger.

'Hello, Marco, how are you?'

Caroline mouthed 'Waiter Marco? You're kidding me!'

'Why, yes. I'd be delighted,' said Tanya. 'Wednesday night? Let me check my diary.' She held the phone at arm's length for ten seconds, grinning at Caroline. 'Yes, I'm free. My flat mate has an evening class. She usually stays out late with her friends at the pub afterwards, so why don't you come round here?'

Caroline looked at the ceiling and shook her head.

'I can order something in for us. ... Excellent. I'll see you then. ... Ciao, bello,' said Tanya.

'Didn't he offer to take you out?'

'Of course he did. But darling, he's a waiter. It's not like he can afford a decent restaurant. I thought I'd be kind and save him the embarrassment. You don't mind about Wednesday, do you?'

'No. Of course not. I'll go to the cinema. At least you didn't tell him you were going to cook and then get me to make a meal for you both.'

Tanya smiled, 'Please. He's just a man. I'm not jeopardising our friendship for him. I'll get the washing up done and then we can finish the movie.'

After Tanya went to bed, Caroline sat on the sofa.

Typical. Tanya had lovely Jimmy, now she was going to have the gorgeous Marco and she'd get the job in London. Of course she would. Particularly as she wouldn't have a chance to feed her the daffodil bulbs.

Caroline took a chocolate mousse from the fridge, tipped it into a bowl—and added double cream.

On Wednesday night, at six o'clock, on her way to get her coat to go home, Caroline passed Jimmy's cubicle. He was staring at his screen, scrolling through a long list of support calls in his name. Well, there were worse ways to spend the evening than helping him out. Helping Jimmy would be her good deed for the day, and perhaps there would be a chance to warn him about Tanya and Marco.

'Crikey, Jimmy, do you need a hand?'

He swung round in his chair.

'Oh. It's you. No, I can manage, thank you.' He looked angry and turned back to face the screen.

She moved her mouth, trying for coherent speech. Instead, she felt a blush of humiliation burning her cheeks. She was only trying to help and the ungrateful bastard had just snubbed her. He was probably hoping for Tanya to magically appear or call. Hard luck matey.

Caroline stalked from him and hoped the cinema was showing a really good horror movie, with a female lead who'd butcher scantily clad young men.

At ten-thirty Caroline left the cinema, after watching a British romantic comedy. It lightened her mood, as the girl wasn't an elf-like creature, but had a rounded figure like her own.

The night was clear, with a half moon. She decided to walk home and she crossed the road to the park.

There were no lights, so the frosty grass was moonlit, prompting her to think of fairyland. She wanted to enjoy it as much as possible, so she slowed her pace.

Tears welled in her eyes as she realised how close to hurting Tanya she'd come, and how much she'd miss her when she left for London. She'd be free and very alone.

On the far side of the park, five minutes from home; the street lights came through the trees, lighting the path.

Someone spoke angrily, and she saw a man standing on the grass with a mobile phone.

'Please, just pick up,' he said. 'I only want to talk. I know you're there. I saw the lights.'

She hesitated, wondering if she should turn back. He ended the call and then redialed. Caroline walked on, concentrating on the path and not looking at him.

'Tanya, please,' he said. 'I need to talk to you; I need to be with you. Please!'

Now he'd mentioned Tanya, she recognised the voice.

'Jimmy?' she said. 'Is that you?'

Jimmy looked at her and laughed.

'Of course. It's fucking Caroline. What? Are you following me? Why can't you leave me ... leave us alone?'

He put the phone in his pocket, turned and walked away from her, towards the children's swings.

Caroline stood for a moment. She stuck her tongue out at his receding back and left the park.

Caroline walked into the house five minutes later. The message light flashed on the phone base. The receiver was off the hook and a recorded voice asked her to replace the handset.

She listened for noises from the bedroom above her, but it was quiet. Tanya and Marco must have finished. She wondered if they were spooning or sleeping at the edges of the bed.

Caroline pressed a button on the phone.

'You have twenty-four unplayed messages.'

They were all from Jimmy.

At first she listened to the messages all the way through, but after the sixth one, she decided it was just too embarrassing. He decayed from friendly and cheerful through concerned to frustrated, then to bewildered and finally, desperate—saying he loved Tanya. The calls she'd overheard in the park weren't the last. There were a couple where he'd hung up without speaking, though Caroline thought she could hear whimpering and sobs.

She returned the receiver to the cradle and followed the cable, to unplug the phone at the wall.

The phone rang. Caroline bit her lower lip. It could be her mother calling. She cautiously lifted the receiver.

'Hello,' she said.

A couple of seconds silence on the line.

'Can I speak to Tanya please?' Jimmy sounded much younger than he was. He could be a teenager, nervous about speaking to his girlfriend's parents.

'She's asleep, Jimmy.'

'Listen Caroline, I know you're lying for her. She may have even told you to, but please, I need to speak to her. Please.'

'Jimmy, really, she's gone to bed.'

'Well, can't you wake her? I won't be long. I promise.'

Caroline thought about this.

'Hello,' said Jimmy. 'Are you there?'

'Listen, Jimmy. She should have told you herself. But honestly, I don't think she loves you. You'd really better find someone else.'

'No. You're lying again. She does love me. She said so. Put her on the phone, or do I have to come round there?'

'Jimmy, please. I'm really sorry, but she isn't alone. There's someone with her.'

She waited for him to scream, to shout at her. She pressed the handset closer to her ear and heard him groan.

'Jimmy, please go home, go to bed and get some rest. Honestly, you'll feel better in the morning.'

Who was she trying to kid? He was behaving as if this was his first love. He'd probably walk around in shock for the next couple of days.

'Jimmy, are you there? Are you OK?' She thought of holding him to her, comforting him. He was good looking and now very vulnerable. He might need her. Perhaps she could go back to the park and find him.

Blushing at her desperation, she ended the call. She would not take one of Tanya's cast-offs.

She unplugged the phone at the wall, checked the doors and windows were securely locked and went to bed.

Caroline slept badly and rose late. She put on her flowery nylon dressing gown and went downstairs.

Tanya was eating breakfast when she walked into the kitchen.

'No Marco?' Caroline said, as she took a cereal bowl from a cupboard.

'He didn't stay.'

'I'm sorry. What?'

'He didn't stay the night.' Tanya smiled. 'I asked him to leave and like a gentleman, he did.'

'Why? Did he snore?'

'No,' Tanya said. 'I was getting a lot of phone calls from Jimmy, so I could hardly pretend I was completely unattached and that put a damper on things. You saw I left the phone off the hook?'

Caroline nodded as she added cereal to the bowl and placed it on the table.

'Besides, Marco said he doesn't sleep with women on the first date.'

'So, you didn't ask him to leave, he left of his own accord?'

Tanya grimaced. 'Yes. I was surprised. I mean he was really nice about it and he wants to see me again.'

'So, what about Jimmy?'

Caroline opened the fridge door and reached for a glass milk bottle.

'I think I should take him more seriously,' said Tanya.

Caroline froze, her finger tips about to grasp the bottle. She didn't dare look at Tanya.

'I'm sorry, what did you say?'

'When I talked to Marco, I realised Jimmy really cares about me. Why else would he call so many times? And he makes me laugh. I like that. I like his Welsh accent.' She looked at Caroline's back. 'Perhaps I got scared that falling in love with Jimmy would be difficult, would make my career plan change. Moving to London would be complicated.'

Caroline pulled her dressing gown tighter round her throat. She thought the fridge must be set too low, as the air from it was so cold her breath was frosting. She took hold of the milk bottle and lifted it from the door.

'Actually,' said Tanya. 'I think I'm a bit … more than a bit, in love with Jimmy.'

Caroline felt the bottle move in her hand. It smashed on the floor, splashing her bare ankles in cold milk.

'Shit, shit!'

'Are you OK?' said Tanya. She stood up and took a cloth from beside the sink. 'I'm sorry, I didn't mean to startle you.'

'Oh, this is bad,' said Caroline.

'It's just spilled milk. Literally, nothing to cry over. You get in the shower—'

'No, listen. I spoke to Jimmy last night. I thought Marco was still here I … I … I told him, you weren't alone.'

Tanya frowned. 'Why would you do that?'

'I'm sorry, I didn't mean … it's just that he was in the park last night and it was late and he said he was going to come round here if I didn't let him speak to you … I'm really sorry.'

Tanya looked at her for a few moments and then half smiled. 'You pranny. Honestly, you do like to make my life difficult.'

'I'll tell him,' said Caroline. 'I mean it's my fault.'

'No, no. You've done enough. But listen, I'm sure he'll understand once I've spoken to him. I mean, I know he's sensitive, he'll have been hurt, but … oh, crap. Look at the time. Order a taxi for 7.40 from here to the office; I can catch him before he starts work.'

Tanya called Jimmy's mobile as she was getting ready, but it went to voicemail.

Jimmy wasn't at his desk. Tanya stayed as long as she could, and made Caroline promise to let her know as soon as he arrived. She went to her office to prepare for the promotion interview.

Every fifteen minutes, Caroline stood to look over her cubicle to see if Jimmy had arrived.

At ten o'clock, two men wearing suits and visitor badges entered the department with Caroline's boss, Siobhan Hegerty. They went into her office. Caroline watched as Siobhan closed her door and angled the blinds in a floor to ceiling window beside it, to give them privacy. Caroline saw Jimmy reflected in the window, coming into the office behind her.

'Jimmy,' she said as she swung her chair to face him.

He wasn't there. A couple of her colleagues followed her gaze.

'Are you alright, Caroline?' said Amy, a motherly woman in her forties, who sat next to her.

Caroline laughed quietly. 'I must be seeing things. I could have sworn Jimmy had just come in.'

'No-one there, lovely,' said Amy. 'Are you sure you're alright? You're shivering.'

'What? No … yes, I'm fine.' Caroline took the cardigan she kept on the back of her chair and put it on.

Siobhan came out of her office.

'Caroline, please come to my office. My visitors would like to speak with you.'

Caroline pulled her cardigan round her and followed Siobhan. When she'd spoken to the visitors, she must remember to mention the air conditioning was too cold.

Both men stood as she entered Siobhan's office. The older one shook her hand.

'Hello, Miss Lampard. My name is Detective Sergeant Purbeck and this is my colleague, Detective Constable Richards. I'm sorry to disturb you, but we need to ask you a few questions about James Marten. Please, take a seat.' He looked at Siobhan. 'Thank you for letting us use your office Mrs Hegerty. We won't be long.'

Siobhan nodded and left the room, closing the door behind her. Caroline sat in a chair at a small conference table.

'Miss Lampard,' said Purbeck. 'When did you last see or speak to Mr Marten.'

'Jimmy? I saw him last night, in Horsham Park, around ten-thirty.'

Richards was making notes, so she waited for him to stop writing.

'Did you speak to him?' said Purbeck.

'Not then, no.'

'But, you did speak to him last night.'

'Yes, he phoned when I got back to the house.'

For a moment she considered asking him what had happened to Jimmy, but she'd worked it out and by *not* asking perhaps it wouldn't be true.

'What did you talk about?' said Purbeck.

She looked down at her lap.

'He was asking to speak to Tanya, my housemate, they'd been seeing each other, but it was late and I said … I said …'

Richards looked up from his notebook.

'What precisely did you say, Miss Lampard?' said Purbeck.

'I said that Tanya was sleeping with Marco, but I was wrong, she wasn't … I didn't mean … He's hurt himself, hasn't he?'

'I'm afraid so, yes,' said Purbeck.

'How? What did he do?'

'We can't discuss that now.'

'I hanged myself in the children's play area.'

Caroline looked at Richards, assuming it was he who'd spoken.

'Why the children's play area?' said Caroline.

The men looked at each other, then at her.

'I'm sorry, Miss,' said Richards. 'Did you ask me why the children's play area?'

'Yes, you just said he'd hanged himself in the children's play area.'

'No. I didn't speak.'

Caroline looked at their faces, which showed concern, then suspicion.

'How did you know about the children's play area?' said Purbeck. 'Did you walk through the park and see the police tape, Miss?'

'No. We came by taxi.'

'It was difficult. I used the chains on one of the swings.'

Caroline watched both men as she listened to Jimmy's voice.

'I'm sorry,' said Caroline. 'I can hear—'

'Sshh. Our secret.'

'I don't think I can talk to you now,' said Caroline.

The policemen looked at each other and then stood.

'As you wish, Miss,' said Purbeck. 'I think we have all we need at the moment. We'll be in touch about you giving a formal statement. You won't need to come to the police station; we can come to your home. At some point, in a few months, you'll probably be called as a witness at the Coroner's Inquest.'

Both men left and Caroline wasn't sure if she was supposed to follow them, or wait for Siobhan to come back. She waited for a minute in the room, listening for Jimmy's voice.

Siobhan opened the door.

'You look ... I think you'd better go home, Caroline,' said Siobhan. 'But can you wait until I've told everyone?'

Caroline nodded, and walked back to her cubicle. She noticed that Betty from HR was standing outside Siobhan's office.

'Everyone!' said Siobhan. 'Please end your current call, switch your phone to silent and come over here please.' The dozen members of the department did as they were asked and gathered round her.

'I'm sorry to have to tell you that James Marten ... I mean Jimmy, was found dead this morning, in Horsham Park.' She waited for the sounds of shock to die down. 'The police aren't saying how he died, but they aren't looking for anyone else in connection with his death. They've asked me to say they may need to interview some of you. I'm sure you'll give them the help they need. We'll now have a minute's silence for Jimmy.'

Caroline dropped her head forward and closed her eyes.

'I wasn't sure if I'd break my neck or choke to death.'

'Huh!' said Caroline.

Siobhan scowled at her.

'Thank you everyone,' said Siobhan at the end of the minute. 'I shall be having a meeting with Betty for the next half hour. After that, I'll cancel all meetings for the rest of the day and my door will be open for anyone who wants to talk or has any questions.'

She went into her office with Betty and closed the door.

'They were sacking him,' said Amy.

'What?' said Caroline.

'He told me yesterday,' said Amy. 'He wasn't hitting his performance targets.' She looked at Siobahn's office. 'They must be working on a statement, to ensure they can't be blamed.'

Caroline felt relieved. 'Poor Jimmy. It must have been terrible for him, no wonder ...'

'Seriously? You think you get off that easily, bitch? I did it after what you told me about Marco!'

Amy frowned as she watched Caroline duck her head and flap her hand at her ear, driving off an invisible wasp.

'I'm going home,' said Caroline. 'Siobhan said I should.'

She grabbed her bag and coat, and scurried from the office, wondering why she wasn't crying.

It was drizzling outside, making the pavement slippery. Caroline stopped to put on her coat, blocking the entrance, as she decided what to do, until someone politely asked her to move.

Tanya would still be in her interview, unless the police had interrupted it. There were no messages on her mobile. She didn't want to be in the house by herself, so she walked carefully on the wet pavements to the bookshop and the café, to wait for Tanya's lunch break.

At the café, she was grateful to find Marco wasn't working. She ordered coffee walnut cake and a mocha, and held the cup in two hands as she was trembling.

For half an hour she concentrated, listening for Jimmy. He didn't speak, so she decided the shock was receding. A hot bath would make her feel better so she headed home.

It was still drizzling and each step felt unsafe. Her route meant crossing Albion Way, the dual carriage way around the town centre. There was an underpass, but it led to the park, so she walked to a pelican crossing and pressed the button. The *WAIT* sign illuminated. Her phone vibrated in her bag and she rummaged for it.

A weight pushed against her shoulders and she stumbled forward into the road. A car horn blared. Looking to her right, she saw the terrified face of a woman driver hunched over the steering wheel of a car as it skidded at her.

Caroline froze. The edge of the car's bumper grazed her shins, knocking her down.

Hands touched her, voices asked benign questions of concern, but these just angered her. Blinking, she struggled to her feet and looked round to see who had attacked her.

'Who pushed me?' said Caroline. 'Did anyone see who pushed me?'

The people looked at each other.

'You were alone,' said the driver. 'You just fell forward, there wasn't anyone standing near you.'

'She's right, Miss,' said a young man. 'We saw you and you were alone.' He looked at the woman standing with him. She nodded.

'Perhaps you slipped on the curb,' he said.

Caroline stared at him and then heard the beeps to indicate it was safe to cross the road.

'I'm sorry, my mistake, I have to get home,' said Caroline. Ignoring everyone, she checked for traffic and as nothing was coming on the other carriageway, hurried across the road.

'Nearly got you that time. You'll have to be more careful.'

Caroline stopped and looked around her. There was no-one near so she spoke aloud.

'Jimmy, is that you?'

'None other. You look a mess; bloody shins, torn tights … but you're still walking. Shame. I really wanted you in a wheelchair.'

Caroline looked down at her legs. Her shins were badly grazed and she realised her palms were also shredded and bleeding. Her left elbow hurt and she guessed she'd have a large bruise in the morning.

She felt groggy and wanted to sit down, but there was nowhere close by. The rain fell harder and she felt more uncertain of her footing in her shoes. Barefoot, she walked home, head bowed to avoid people's glances; listening for the sound of Jimmy's voice and conscious of the cold wind and rain on the nape of her neck.

Caroline was in the bath when she heard the front door open.

'Caroline, are you there?' called Tanya.

Her footsteps on the stairs were slow and heavy. She tried the locked door to the bathroom.

'Let me in. Please. I want to talk.'

Carefully, Caroline pushed herself out of the water and the mounds of bubbles in the bath. She didn't normally use bubble bath, but she thought Jimmy might be watching and had felt very naked.

Scenarios of her falling in the tub, or as she stepped onto the wet bathroom floor – pulled by chilly, unseen hands – played in her mind. She wrapped a towel round herself before she opened the door, and then sat on the edge of the bath.

Tanya looked at the floor as she entered, rehearsing in her head what she was about to say. Raising her eyes she saw the wounds on Caroline's shins.

'What happened to you?'

'I got hit by a car. I ... I was thinking about Jimmy.'

'Jesus, it's your hands too. And your elbow ... and you've put dressings on your hands before you got in the bath.' Tanya sighed and opened the cabinet with the first aid kit. 'Take off the towel, let's see the damage.'

Caroline did as she was told, turning when instructed, so Tanya could check for bruising. In silence, Tanya diligently dried and dressed her wounds.

'Thank you,' said Caroline. 'You were going to say something when you came in.'

'It's nothing, really. It's just that I've invited Marco to come to the funeral with me. He's going to stay the night before.'

'Do you know when the funeral is?'

'No. Not yet, but I just wanted ...'

Tanya left and Caroline looked at the mirror, which was covered in steam. Her teeth ached at the sound of an invisible finger as it wrote "BITCHES" across it.

Over the weekend, Caroline listened for Jimmy's voice; scanned shop windows for his reflection and refused to cook, not wanting to spend time in the house. She slept badly, fearing she'd dream of him, fearing his silence meant he was watching and planning how to cripple her.

On the Monday, in the six minute appointment Caroline had with her doctor, she cried, told him about Jimmy's voice and asked if she was going mad.

The doctor smiled encouragingly. 'Honestly, I think it's just stress,' he said. 'You obviously feel guilty, but you didn't make him commit suicide. Listen, you mustn't blame yourself. I'll prescribe some medication to help you sleep and if you're still feeling bad in a week, come back and we can talk further. Perhaps you can take a holiday, get away for a while and put this behind you.' He gave her a leaflet on bereavement.

Caroline thanked him and got the pills from the pharmacy.

As the funeral approached, she planned how to avoid it. She'd hoped it would be held in Wales, but it was going to be at the crematorium in Crawley, nine miles away. Jimmy's parents had recently retired to a village near Horsham, to be closer to Jimmy's sister, who had a newborn.

The evening before the funeral, the Wednesday after Jimmy had died, Caroline prepared a meal whilst Tanya dressed in her room, readying for Marco's arrival.

As Tanya applied lipstick using the mirror on her dressing table, she saw movement out of the corner of her eye. Angling her head to see clearly, she saw Jimmy smiling over her shoulder. She panicked for a moment and then looked more closely as the image changed from Jimmy to Caroline.

She shook her head. The digital frame on top of her chest of drawers, reflected in her mirror, showed a photo of her and Caroline on holiday in Paris.

There were at least a half dozen photos of Jimmy on the frame she could easily remember, and she thought there might be more. She considered deleting them all, but it felt callous. Perhaps after the funeral. She switched the frame off.

Ten minutes later, the doorbell rang. Marco had brought flowers for Tanya and a small box of chocolates for Caroline.

The conversation was subdued at dinner and afterwards Caroline insisted she'd do the washing up.

Upstairs, in her bed, Tanya was thinking about Jimmy as she stroked Marco's hair. She didn't want to, but her thoughts kept fracturing and returning to him.

'What are you thinking?' said Marco, stopping his kissing of her breast.

'I'm sorry ... I ...'

He moved his face to above hers and stroked her hair.

'It's OK, we can just lie here, if you want.'

'No, please ... I need ... you.'

'Si.'

He kissed her passionately, moving his hand between her legs to stroke and tease her.

He smiled at her as she gasped and writhed. The pleasure coruscated through her, pushing Jimmy out of her mind. She wanted this; wanted Marco to enter her and stroke and thrust all the regret away.

She opened the top drawer of her bedside cabinet. For a few moments she fumbled, but eventually she found the condom's silver packet. Marco looked across at her hand.

'Of course,' he said.

He took the packet from her, tore the edge in his teeth, opened it and rolled it on in an easy move. She smiled at the practice this indicated. He wouldn't be hurt when she didn't call after the funeral.

His entry made her groan, it was so teasingly slow and she rolled her head to the side as he kissed and nibbled her neck.

Jimmy's face looked down at her and she gasped. The damn digital frame had turned itself on.

Marco's rhythm increased. She looked to the ceiling, but she had to look back.

Jimmy leered at her. That didn't make sense, the frame didn't contain video.

As Jimmy ran his tongue over his lips, she noticed his right shoulder. It was moving quickly, matching Marco's rhythm. She felt revolted. He was here, watching them.

Jimmy's lips became blue and his eyes opened wide.

Tanya wanted Marco to stop, but not stop. She felt the beginning of her orgasm and wanted to close her eyes so she could enjoy it; but she had to watch Jimmy. Blood oozed from the corner of his eyes; the eyeballs bloated, as if thumbs were pushing them from inside his skull. The whole of his face turned blue, then darkened. He gurgled—how could she hear him? He choked, and as Marco climaxed Jimmy's mouth opened and his black and thickened tongue protruded, filling his mouth, swelling until it touched the edges of the frame and the screen went black.

Tanya thrashed her head from side to side as orgasm wracked her and she bucked beneath Marco, wanting the pleasure to obliterate what she thought she'd seen. She heard Jimmy's laughter.

Marco withdrew, rolled off her onto his back to catch his breath.

Tanya was still for a moment then felt the weight of a cold body on her. She writhed as she felt cold hands stroke and caress her skin and between her legs.

Marco looked across and wondered if she was having a fit. He sat up in bed, fumbling for a light switch. He abandoned the search so he could wrap his arms around her as she sobbed and clung to him.

'You're cold,' he said.

He held her until she fell asleep.

The sun rose on a deep frost which made the roads icy.

Tanya had booked a black car, with driver, to take them to the funeral. It arrived promptly at nine o'clock. Caroline naturally assumed she would travel up front, leaving the back seat for the other two. She was touched the driver insisted on opening the door for her.

Before turning on the engine, the driver checked the route on the satnav.

'We'll have to go through the centre of town,' he said. 'There are delays on the bypass; a lorry's jack-knifed on the ice.'

Tanya frowned. 'At this time of day, it'll be packed.'

'Well, we could go via Wimblehurst, but that means we might get stuck at the level crossing on Parsonage Road.'

'We'll have to risk it,' said Tanya.

'As you wish, Miss.'

'Yes! I mean I can't be late for my own funeral, can I?'

Caroline bit her lower lip.

'It's alright Caroline, you don't have to talk out loud. After all I'm just a figment of your guilt, which you can banish with pills. Aren't I?'

'Can we have some music, please,' said Caroline.

'It's hardly appropriate,' said Tanya.

'People do, Miss,' said the driver. 'I've got a disc of classical music, appropriate like. It's got Satie, Pachelbel, Bach etc. It's already in the machine.'

'Fine,' said Tanya.

Marco squeezed her hand, but she didn't look at him. The driver started the disc from controls on the steering wheel. The first track was Barber's *Adagio for Strings*.

At the level crossing in Parsonage Road a queue of a dozen cars waited for a train to speed past.

The signal lights stopped flashing and the barriers rose. The cars moved forward.

'This is great music to die by.'

You mean be cremated by. You're already dead, thought Caroline.

'Well, see, I can control temperature, right? What if I caused the battery to fail? Right about …'

The car moved onto the crossing and straddled both tracks.

'… now.'

The engine died.

'What's happened?' said Tanya.

'I don't know, Miss,' said the driver as he turned the key. The engine didn't respond and behind them car horns sounded.

'I'll get out and push us. Do you mind helping me, Sir?' He pulled on the door handle, but the lock didn't open.

'And what if I froze all the door locks?'

They released their seat belts and pushed at the doors.

The bells, warning of an approaching train, clanged and they saw the barriers descend. Tanya searched for her phone as they heard the wail of a train horn.

'Jimmy, please. Don't do this,' said Caroline.

The driver reached across her and opened the glove box, to get at the windscreen hammer.

'Why not? It's perfect. All three of you dying, terrified. I reckon Marco's going to piss his pants soon.'

'He's not part of this,' said Caroline, looking at the driver. 'You don't want to kill him, Jimmy.'

The train horn sounded again, and they felt the car rock as other drivers tried to pull open the doors or push the car off the track.

Caroline listened for Jimmy, ignoring the shouts warning the rescuers to save themselves.

The driver found the hammer and raised it to strike the windscreen.

'Turn the key,' said Caroline.

The driver looked at her briefly, decided she was insane and lifted the hammer to smash the windscreen.

Caroline reached across him and turned the ignition key. The engine started.

'Drive,' she said.

Rescuers scattered as the engine roared and the driver pushed hard on the accelerator. The car jumped forward and stopped.

'Again,' said Caroline.

The driver turned the key and the engine started. This time he pushed more gently on the accelerator and the car moved forward as, with brakes screeching, the train passed behind them.

It was during his sister's eulogy that Caroline saw Jimmy. He stood beside the coffin, which rested on the catafalque. He wasn't pale, or see-through. He looked real and was dressed like other mourners in a black suit and tie, with a white shirt. He stared at his coffin, stroked it, and glanced at his sister when she faltered, or got a laugh.

He looked bewildered and when the celebrant signalled the curtains should be drawn round the coffin, he went to him and screamed, 'No! You can't do this! I'm still here! They'll burn me!'

He looked around the chapel and locked eyes with Caroline.

'You can see me, can't you? Tell them!'

Caroline took a tissue from her bag and wiped her eyes. 'I'm sorry,' she said quietly into the hanky, hoping no-one would notice her speak.

Jimmy walked towards her, shouting obscenities. She pushed past two other mourners to get out of the row before Jimmy could block her in, and ran to the door.

She felt the cold of Jimmy's breath on the back of her neck as she ran deep into the gardens of remembrance. Then he was gone. She turned to walk back to the others, but took a wrong turn. The garden she entered had a high hedge and memorials next to standard rose bushes. Jimmy sat on his haunches, examining one of the small stone markers.

'I thought you'd gone,' said Caroline.

Jimmy looked up at her. 'Like, up in a puff of smoke you mean?'

'No. I didn't mean ...' She looked back at the crematorium and the chimney above the trees. 'I guess you don't want to be around when they … Look, I'm sorry. I don't know what to say and I don't think any of your family are going to believe me, if I tell them I can see you.'

Jimmy stood and walked away from her a few paces.

'There's no bloody proper memorials here,' he said. 'No proper grave stones, just rocks and a few bloody bushes. Not like the Victorians, they knew how to put up a proper monument. They showed that someone had lived, see?'

'Yeah, if you had a lot of money.'

Jimmy scowled at her and folded his arms. She waited for him to speak, but he was staring at the chimney.

'You look very nice, in your suit. I didn't expect you to …'

'Dress nicely, for my own funeral? Do you think I should look more like some Dickensian spirit, or like this?'

He rose a couple of feet into the air and his clothes changed to those he was wearing on the night he died. He pulled at a chain wrapped around his neck, as his head twisted to one side. His legs kicked in his death throes, his face showing his panic as he struggled to save himself.

'Stop, please,' she said.

'OK, how do you like this?'

Jimmy vanished his clothes, except for striped boxer shorts and hung in the air like the crucified Christ. 'Better?' he said.

Caroline looked round her for a path back to the crematorium. Jimmy stepped down through the air, clothing himself in the suit and shirt.

'You can't escape me,' he said. 'You probably always thought we ghosts were frozen to the place where we died, carrying our heads under our arms. Think, if you didn't have a body, how quickly would you learn to transform how people saw you? That's the trouble, see?

Ghost stories are written by the living and you know fuck all about being dead.'

He grabbed her chin in one hand, twisting her head to scan the garden as he stepped behind her. His icy fingers were so cold they burned her skin.

'Look around you, can you see them?' said Jimmy.

'No. See who?'

'All the dead. We don't go anywhere, see. There's no Heaven. No Hell. No Nirvana, Happy Hunting Ground and no Valhalla. Just here, all the dead wandering the world, watching the living; waiting for you to join us. We're addicted to the living.'

He let her go, walked to a tree and leaned against it, watching the chimney.

'Ghosts meet, fall in love and don't have children. They watch their living children and grandchildren grow. Those that don't take an interest, well, they freeze, become statues. That phrase, when you feel a sudden chill. It's not someone walking on your grave; it's you walking through one of them.'

He pulled a pack of cigarettes from his pocket and lit one. He watched the cigarette smoke.

'Enough of death, let's speak of love,' he said. He smiled ruefully at her. 'I hardly recognised myself, after I fell for Tanya. My chest felt tight, I wanted to cry all the time, but I don't cry. Rugby players don't—unless we miss the goal, win or lose. Waiting for her to call, checking my phone for messages and the battery, paranoid if I didn't have a charger on me. Looking for her. Always looking for her, see? That twist in the stomach when I spoke to her, a happy glow which lasted until I wondered when we'd next speak. Obsessed, I was.'

'It's not a kind of magic—it's a kind of madness, isn't it? Believing only they can make you happy.'

He sneered at her. 'Very profound, that is. A real Hallmark sentiment. I know what I felt ... *we* felt and she loved me.'

Caroline blushed.

'I do know what you mean, you know,' she said. 'I danced with a boy. At a school dance, he smiled at me. I thought it was going to be like *Carrie*, the film? That it was a set up and they'd all laugh at me, but it wasn't, he actually liked—'

'I don't fucking care! Do you understand? You have to help me get her back. ... That night, when I was calling her, I told myself she needed me. I thought we could have a baby, to make up for the one she lost, at university.'

'She told you about that?' said Caroline.

'Of course she did. Why wouldn't she? I told you, she loved me. She's the *one.*'

'OK, I believe you. So, what do you want me to do? Hold a séance?'

'Quite simple, really. All you have to do—'

Caroline's phone rang.

'I'm sorry, that'll be her.' She found the phone in her bag. 'Hello? ... Yes, sorry. I'm in the gardens, I got lost, but I'll find my way back.' She ended the call.

She looked round to find Jimmy standing a few inches from her. There was nothing boyish about his face now, nothing sorrowful—just determination.

'You're going to kill her, so we can be together. Forever, and ever and ever. Romantic, isn't it?'

In the car home, Caroline answered questions only in monosyllables.

After they'd dropped Marco at the bookshop, Tanya said she'd take a shower when they got in and then try to get some sleep.

Caroline filled the kettle at the kitchen sink. A cold breeze stroked the back of her neck.

'When will you poison her?' said Jimmy.

'I've been thinking about it and I won't do it. I won't kill her.'

'Seriously? You know you want to. I saw the way you looked at her when I was alive. You're jealous of her and it'll be so easy. I know you've done the research; I've seen that book under your pillow and the daffodil bulbs.'

'I know. But your death, it's brought us closer. Reminded me of what's important.'

'And you think that's it, do you? You two are happy and I'll just fade away.'

'What are you going to do to me? Make the room chilly? Fine, I'll put on a jumper. Or kill me? Cripple me? I'll get you exorcised and you'll never see Tanya. You'll never have her, Jimmy.'

He gave her a slow hand clap.

'Bravo, Caroline. You've got more guts than I thought. Let's see now. You want to prevent me from seeing my true love. I wonder if I can return the favour.'

Jimmy turned from her and walked towards the front door, fading as he went. Then he stopped and looked at her over his shoulder, grinning.

'Very Cheshire Cat,' she said, as he vanished.

Caroline didn't feel hungry at lunch time, and was deciding on the evening meal when Tanya came downstairs at five o'clock.

'Do you want tea?' said Caroline.

'Yes, please. What do you want to do about dinner? I can order in a Chinese, if you don't want to cook.'

'I'm not that hungry,' said Caroline. 'There's a packet of risotto in the cupboard. Will that do?'

'Yeah. Fine.'

Caroline added a sprig of parsley from the kitchen windowsill to the mushroom risotto, before placing the dishes on the table. Tanya started eating. Caroline stared at her plate, her throat tight. Amongst the rice, maggots writhed and chewed on each other. Maggot innards spewed from the wounds.

She looked across at Tanya's plate, which was half empty. Her risotto looked fine.

Tanya noticed her staring. 'What's wrong?' she said.

'Nothing,' said Caroline. 'I've just lost my appetite.'

'Well, if you don't want yours, I'll eat it. I'm ravenous.'

Jimmy stood behind Tanya.

'I wonder how long you'll last Caroline. I mean, you've got all that blubber you carry round, so I guess it'll be a week or two. But you'll need water. Shame you won't like the taste.' He mimed undoing his zip and pissing into a glass.

He pulled a face of mock sympathy.

'You know what you need to do, if you want to eat again, don't you? Though you'd best be careful how you do it, otherwise the only food you'll be eating will be in prison.'

The next day Caroline called in sick. She couldn't take the remaining pills the doctor had prescribed, as that needed water and – as Jimmy had predicted – all liquids stank, and tasted, of rancid urine. Google said she had three days to survive without water.

She spent the first day sorting an exorcism. Not a church goer, she didn't bother with the Catholic or Anglian church websites. Others offering exorcisms were all American. They could perform the exorcism remotely or fly to her for expenses. Caroline didn't have enough money for the tickets and they wouldn't get to her in time. Pacing her room, she remembered a shop specialising in New Age paraphernalia in the centre of town, so she walked there.

There were a lot of fairies, angels, unicorns and pictures of rainbows in the window of the shop. She waited outside, wanting there to be no-one else inside when she spoke to someone. Two teenage girls left so she entered.

The opening door knocked some chimes and the sound made her jump.

A middle-aged woman was behind the counter. She wore small round glasses, a loose knitted jumper with a rainbow pattern, and a scarf around her head, knotted at the side with a length draping down her shoulder.

'What can I do for you both?' she said.

Caroline looked around her. She was alone.

'I'm sorry, it's just me.'

The woman looked surprised, then squinted at Caroline. She took off her glasses, breathed on them and polished them with the scarf.

'How odd. I could have sworn … Must have been a trick of the shadows. Well, how can I help, dear?'

'I want an exorcism. I'm being haunted.'

The woman raised her eyebrows.

'You mean your house is haunted. Ghosts, *if* they exist, don't haunt people. They haunt places.'

'But I thought you'd believe in ghosts.'

'Me dear, no. I believe in angels and guiding spirits, ancient woodland folk and gods, but ghosts—no. I think the dead are reborn into a new life. They don't hang around playing peek-a-boo.'

'Fairies, but not ghosts.'

'It depends what you mean by a ghost. If you go into a strange room, you'll look at the decor; perhaps check the books to find out what the owner is like. If I tell you the room is haunted, you'll go in looking for a ghost—hoping you're special enough to see one. You want to be special, part of the story. So you'll do your best to *see* the ghost. That's all ghosts are. Stories, which grow in the telling and we all want to be part of a good story.'

'But I can hear him, and speak to him, and see him. He tried to kill us. Please, I need your help.'

The woman sighed, then turned the sign on the door to show the shop was closed, and locked the door.

'My name's Margaret, I think we'd better have a cup of tea.'

Whilst she made herbal tea, Caroline told her story. Margaret presented her with a mug of steaming camomile tea. One sniff and Caroline had to put the cup down.

'Well, that's quite horrible for you,' said Margaret. 'But I think I can help. There's someone I know, a priest.' She stood and picked up a large address book.

'I think I can kill her,' said Jimmy.

He stood behind Margaret stroking his chin, then flicked his hand. A breeze moved a carousel of cellophane cards. Margaret looked at the door.

'Honestly, that door. I really must seal it properly against the wind.'

Jimmy surveyed the shop. 'Hmm. Cards won't do, what I need is … ah, there we are.'

He moved to a display of envelopes and coloured writing paper and blew on them. Margaret stared, slack-jawed, as they fountained into the air. Instead of falling, they swirled in a tornado near the ceiling.

'He's here, isn't he?' said Margaret.

'Yes, he wants to … to hurt you.'

'Fundamenta eius in montibus sanctis!' shouted Margaret, raising her arms.

Jimmy laughed. 'Tell your friend I know that one. Others have told me about it. She remembers it from a Dennis Wheatley novel, or the movie. It doesn't work.'

Jimmy pointed at the sheets circling at the ceiling and then flicked his finger towards Margaret. Sheets of paper flew at her. The edge of one cut her cheek, then another near her right brow. The paper twisted around her, diving at her face like a flock of seagulls tearing flesh from a carcass on the shore. She put her hands over her eyes, but Jimmy pulled them away so the paper could fly at them.

Margaret screamed in pain and terror as her vision clouded.

'Jimmy, please leave her alone!'

'Then leave and don't listen to her.'

Caroline opened the door and ran from the shop. Behind her Margaret collapsed to her knees as the paper fell gently around her.

She called for help and a couple walking past entered the shop. Pieces of paper, spattered with blood and vitreous humour, lay on the floor. Margaret knelt amongst them and turned her bloody face to the couple.

'Please help me. I can't see.'

Caroline ran for a couple of hundred yards, but was soon out of breath. She walked to the taxi rank in the Carfax and took a cab home.

She filled a tall glass with water, took it upstairs and put it on her bedside cabinet. She placed a chair so she could reach a large, flat box on top of the wardrobe.

The ivory dress, decorated in fake pearls, had been her mother's, and was folded in tissue paper. Standing in front of her full length mirror, she pulled it on. It didn't fit her and left a gaping 'V' shape at her back.

'What are you doing?' said Jimmy.

He stood behind her, watching her in the mirror.

'I said, "What are you doing?"'

Caroline continued pulling at the dress, to make it fit.

'You really love Tanya, don't you Jimmy?'

'Yes, I bloody do. What are you doing?'

'That's good.'

Caroline sat down on the edge of the bed.

'You know, given a couple of weeks of not eating, I reckon I could fit into this dress. But, as you said, as a ghost I can look how I want. This too solid flesh will melt and I can look like Tanya.'

117

She swallowed the remaining sleeping pills with the water, choking at the taste, and lay down.

She smiled, like any bride on her wedding day.

WHY WON'T THEY TELL ME?

The date is 1st November 1883. I am called Cassie. I am eight years old.

Mama says … Mama *said*: I talk too much and a lot of nonsense, a lot of the time. I also ask too many questions. But how am I to find things out if I don't ask questions? That's what I want to know. Particularly when people are too busy to answer me properly and say I should ask later. Or they say it doesn't concern me. Well, it does concern me or I wouldn't ask the question, would I? I want to know what will happen to me.

I've been told I must write down my story, even though the nasty policeman says it is all a pack of lies and I have a wild imagination. He is of the opinion that as I come from "theatrical folk" it is only to be expected. I don't have a wild imagination. It was Freddy who made up the best stories. I'm writing this for the nice policeman. He says I should write down everything I remember, then "we'll see" what will happen to me.

I suppose I'd best begin at the beginning and go on to the end and then stop. That's the best way to tell a story, according to Mr Lewis Carroll, who wrote the best book in the whole wide world ever.

To begin with, Papa, was very popular in Manchester at The People's Music Hall, which makes me wonder if they built music halls for animals as well.

He was so popular he came to live in London. He got off the train and he fell in love with the girl who sang "The boy I love sends yellow roses", at Wilson's Music

Hall. That was Mama and he sent her yellow roses every day for a week before she'd agree to walk out with him.

Then they got married and then Betty was born, and then Freddy, and then two small boys who are in Heaven, and then me.

My Papa, Jeremiah Turner, sister Betty, aged sixteen and brother Freddy, aged fourteen were "The Three Turners". They were very popular on the music halls. Mama sewed the costumes for the act and she worked back stage, doing the costumes for the chorus girls.

Betty told me that Mama really came to the theatre to keep an eye on Papa and Freddy as: "You know what chorus girls are like." I didn't know, still don't know, what chorus girls are like because "It doesn't concern me," though, apparently, I'll know when I'm older. I know they're "No better than they should be." Maisie, who does an act with dogs, told me. But, honestly, that doesn't make any sense.

P.C. Higgins – P.C. stands for Police Constable – says I should stick to writing the facts, just everything I saw and heard. I've seen and heard a lot of things, as I'm eight years old, but I think he means about last night. I don't want to think about it, but they say I must tell the truth. I keep telling the truth, but I know they don't believe me. That's not fair. When people tell you the truth, you should believe them.

According to P.C. Higgins – he says I can call him Joe – according to Joe, all I have to write down is the facts without "embellishments". He said that word as if I wouldn't know what it meant as it was too long, but I'd often go to the music hall, and the Chairman used lots of long words, as people would go "ooh" and "ah" when he said them. He taught me some of them. Terpsichorean is a word, it means a dancer. He used to say; "My Lords, Ladies and Gentlemen, the Management of the Wilson Music Hall are proud to present those wonders of the terpsichorean art, those marvels of musical melodrama, mystery and romance—I give you, your own, your very own: The Three Turners!"

Then he'd bang his gavel on the table and the audience would applaud and cheer. Papa, Freddy and Betty did complex and humorous dance routines, which Freddy sometimes got wrong. Betty would sing a song. Usually it was something silly about a boy and how she loved him. She sang really beautifully, but she was mean at home.

A week ago, on Sunday, I was playing with my dolly, Rebecca, in front of the parlour fire. Betty, Freddy and Mama were playing a card game. Freddy was winning, though Betty said it was by cheating. I didn't understand how you could cheat at *Happy Families*, but Betty – who insisted we call her Elizabeth, now she was sixteen – said Freddy could find a way to cheat at anything. In her opinion Freddy was a bad lot and would end up on Queer Street.

Freddy just laughed at her. I thought he was much nicer than Betty. At fourteen, he'd often spend time with me, making up stories; about how Rebecca wasn't really a doll with a china head, but a princess who'd been enchanted by an evil witch. He would act out the story for me, playing all the parts. He was particularly good at portraying Bettina, the evil witch—who spoke an awful lot like my sister.

Betty said that she would marry someone rich and, if her children were half as horrible as Freddy and I, then she would have nursemaids and governesses, and that would be a great thing as then she'd hardly ever have to see the brats.

'And where will the likes of you meet such a gentleman?' said Mama.

'Why, when I am a famous star of the stage, they will be queuing to propose to me Mother.'

'Ah, yes!' said Freddy. 'I can see it now, "Miss Betty–"'

Betty glared at him.

'Sorry, Miss Elizabeth Turner, star of the London stage, songstress: famous for her duck impressions: "quack, quack!"'

Betty flung her cards at him.

'Children!' said Mama. 'Clear up this mess. Your father will be home soon. Betty, come to the kitchen as soon as you've finished and help me with the potatoes.'

'It's alright Mother, I'll tidy,' said Freddy, making sure that Betty would leave us as soon as possible. Betty scowled at him and mouthed "I'll get you," as she left the room.

'Freddy, do you think Betty will be famous?' I said.

'Oh, yes. I'm afraid so. Father knows it too. That's why he keeps giving her more to do in the act. You see Cassie, The Three Turners; aren't as popular as we were. I can dance and sing a bit, but I don't love it like Betty, and Father … well, he's been tired a lot recently.'

I knew what "tired" meant. Papa had been staying out with his friends at the pub. I didn't like it when he got home and kissed me goodnight, as his breath smelt of gin and his face had stubble on it most nights.

Papa hadn't returned by the time supper was ready. Mama quietly served our plates and we ate in silence. When Papa came home late on a Sunday, there would probably be shouting and I didn't like that. Betty, Freddy and I knew to go to our room as soon as we could.

About eight o'clock there was a loud knocking on the front door. They knocked four times, slowly. We sat looking at each other. No-one called at the house on a Sunday night and I'm sure we all thought it must be bad news.

They knocked again, louder and faster and that broke the spell. Mama stood, telling us to stay at the kitchen table. We heard her open the door and then Papa's voice.

'What kept you, woman?'

'But the door was unlocked—it always is. Why did you knock?'

'A surprise! Call the children into the parlour. I have great news!'

We didn't need to be called and crowded into the room.

Papa placed two large varnished wood boxes on the table. Each had a brass handle at the top.

'What are those, Harry?' said Mama. I didn't understand why she sounded so doubtful. Papa said they were a surprise and surprises are always nice.

'These are our future, my dear; yours, Cassie's and particularly young Fred's. Wait while I hang my coat and I'll show you.'

The taller of the boxes had latches at the base. He undid these and slowly lifted the top to reveal an oblong box, with two tarnished brass tubes protruding from the front. They had brass covers on them.

'What is it?' I said.

'A magic lantern,' said Papa, whispering the words, just to be dramatic. 'You see these lenses Cassie?' He indicated the brass tubes. 'Well, they're used to make pictures on a screen.'

'But where did it come from?' said Mother.

Papa hesitated before answering.

'Jebediah Havant. They auctioned the contents of the house yesterday and I picked these up today.'

'No, Harry, not that family,' said Mama.

'Hush, woman. They won't be needing them, will they?'

'What is it, what's wrong with the Havant family?' I said.

They all looked very grave.

'Hush now Cassie,' said Mama. 'You don't need to know.'

'Why not?'

'Cassie, be quiet or you'll go to your room,' said Papa.

I knew better than to ask more questions. I could see that Freddy and Betty knew. They would talk about it later, when we were in bed, so I could wait until then.

'I still don't understand Harry. Why have you bought it?'

'Well, lass, it's like this. Management of music hall, well, they no longer require the services of The Three Turners.'

'No!' said Mama, reaching for the back of a chair to steady herself.

'Easy pet, listen will you? That's why I bought the magic lantern. You see our Freddy here, he's a natural born story teller. He can write stories based on the slides and operate the projector, I can tell them and you can play the piano to give the story some drama and for the sing songs between the sets of slides. There's dozens of slides in this chest here and there's another chest to come.'

'What about me, Papa?' said Betty.

'You, my lass, are to be a star! Truth to tell, they didn't want The Three Turners, but you; they do want. Your Mother and I, we'll work up some songs with you.'

Freddy and I looked at each other. Betty was going to be impossible to live with.

I was sent to bed early, as usual, but I stayed awake, waiting for Freddy and Betty to come up. Betty and I shared the big bed and Fred had a bed by the window.

As they came up the stairs, I heard them talking.

'I don't know Fred, some of those slides are pretty gruesome.'

'That's what people want at this time of the year, Betty. It's as Father says, everyone likes a good scare. Even Mr Dickens wrote ghost stories, and these slides … well, they're no worse than you see in the penny dreadfuls.'

'That's my point, Fred, not everyone reads or likes the penny dreadfuls.'

Betty came into the room first, carrying a lighted candle. She sat at the dressing table to brush out her long dark hair.

'What are you doing still awake?'

'I want you to tell me about the Havant family.'

'Don't, Betty,' said Freddy. 'You'll just scare her and then we'll none of us get any sleep.'

'That's true.'

'Why? What happened to them?'

'You know,' said Betty, 'When I'm rich and a star, like Father says, the first thing I'm going to do is tell Father and Mother that you're to be sent away.'

'Steady on, Betty, that's pretty strong, even for you.'

Betty smirked at Freddy.

'I don't see why. I only meant she should be sent to a nice school, somewhere in the country, with all the other noisy little brats.'

'I don't want to go away,' I whispered, shocked at the suggestion.

'We'll see,' said Betty.

'I hate you,' I said, then stuck out my tongue and folded my arms.

Betty laughed. 'The feeling's mutual, I'm sure. Now, go to sleep, I don't want to listen to you anymore.'

Freddy took off his trousers and boots and got into bed.

There was a street lamp outside our window and it cast light into our room, as we left the curtains open to save on candles. It was Freddy's job to pull the curtains closed only when we were all in bed. The light meant that Freddy could make shadow puppets on the wall, where Betty sat at the dressing table. He often did this to amuse me.

That night he made the shadow of a rabbit, then a bird above Betty. It looked as if the bird had landed on her head. Then he sat up in bed to make the shape of a strange hunched man with long spiky fingers and little horns on his head. He made the shadow move across the wall and reach out for Betty. She brushed her hair and didn't notice the shadow's hands reach for her throat.

I tried not to giggle too loudly.

Betty started coughing and then she was choking.

I turned to look at Freddy. He was scared, as his hands were by his side clutching the covers—he wasn't casting the shadow!

He turned in his bed, to look outside the window and I looked too. There was nothing there, just the street lamp.

Betty was choking and the shadow of the man was still there, strangling her.

I started to cry as I was scared.

Freddy pulled the curtain across the windows and the only light was from the candle on the dresser. Betty coughed and then took a few deep breaths.

Freddy and I checked Betty's shadow, cast by her candle. It was just her.

'I'm sorry, I'm sorry!' I said. 'I don't want you to die. I don't hate you really, please don't die!'

'What? I'm not dying,' said Betty, though she was still breathing quickly. 'It was just a cough.'

I looked at Freddy and could see he was worried.

'But the shadow demon, he attacked you!' I said.

'Fred, if you've been making fun of me with your shadow puppets, I swear I'll box your ears.

'No, it wasn't Freddy, it wasn't!'

Betty looked at Freddy. He shrugged.

Betty sighed. 'It's alright Cassie, alright.'

She came over and stroked my hair.

'I'm sorry for being mean to you, I was only teasing.'

She kissed the top of my head, undressed and got into bed with me. All the time the candle was lit, I watched the shadows.

The next morning, Betty was in a bad mood again. As she was being mean to me over breakfast I tried to work out if there was enough light in the kitchen to form shadows, but it was too misty outside. I thought I'd have to do some explaining if I asked for candles and the curtains to be drawn closed. I just wondered if I could summon the shadow demon as Freddy had done, to scare Betty.

Papa came in from the parlour with Freddy. They'd been up early to look at the slides and work out stories.

'Now Fred, it were just a coincidence, that's all lad. There ain't no such things as—' He stopped when he caught sight of me practising being a demon with spiky fingers.

He burst out laughing and then pretended to be a monster. I ran squealing and giggling as he chased me round the house.

Later that morning, Mama looked worried as we boarded the omnibus to the music hall. She had to go in to mend some costumes and Papa had said he didn't want me under his feet whilst he and Freddy worked on the slides. Betty was to stay at home and do some housework.

On the omnibus, I learned what had happened to the Havants. There was a man sitting opposite, reading The Illustrated Police News. It was on the front page; how Mr Havant was on trial for murdering his whole family. The pictures showed Mrs Havant and six children—all dead.

At the theatre I visited with James, the stage doorman, whilst Mama was doing her sewing. In James's opinion it was a "sad business about the Havants", particularly as James knew Mr Havant and he thought him a thoroughly respectable and hardworking man.

James said: "Havant ran a magic lantern show underneath the arches at St Pancras station. Very popular they were, too. I happen to know he was working on a new show for Halloween. Very excited about it, he was."

When we got home, Papa and Fred were arguing in the parlour. Betty was listening outside the closed door. She looked guilty when she saw Mama and stood to one side so we could enter.

There were papers strewn around the room and I recognised Freddy's handwriting on them. He and Papa stood facing each other and Papa had another piece of paper, which he was waving in front of Freddy's face.

'Fred lad, you're going to have to better than this, you know.'

'Please, Father. I'm doing my best and not all the slides are here yet. There's three which are obviously from a set we still haven't received. They look the most interesting. These are just some ideas, Father.'

'Well, you'll just have to have better ideas, lad.'

'Harry, give Fred a chance, he's only had a day and you're asking a lot of him,' said Mama. 'I still don't know why you didn't buy the scripts and sheet music.'

'Because it were too much money, pet.'

'What do you mean Harry? How do we not have enough money?'

Papa sank into a chair.

'I was going to tell you pet, you see it's all the other expenses. There's not just the projector and slides, there's adverts in paper, posters, hire of hall with a piano; there's new songs for Betty and new costumes.'

I pulled at Mama's sleeve.

'Mama.'

'Not now, Cassie.' She didn't look down at me.

'Mama! Freddy's bleeding!'

We all looked at Freddy. He was very pale and bright red blood was running from his nose.

'Harry, did you hit Freddy?'

'No pet, I swear.'

Freddy swayed and Papa caught him as he fell. He sat him in a chair.

'Betty, get the key from the back door,' said Papa.

'What for?'

'So we can put it down the back of his neck, what else? Fred lad, keep your head back.'

'Bring me a bowl of cold water and a towel,' said Mama.

'Which first? Key or water?'

Papa looked at Mama.

'Both!' they said together.

Betty threw her arms up in frustration and went to the kitchen.

'Is Freddy going to die?' I said.

'No, it's just a nose bleed,' said Mama. 'Sit quietly whilst we sort out Fred. He'll be fine, you'll see.'

Freddy looked very pale to me.

When Betty came in a couple of minutes later she brought the key, towel and bowl of water, but she too looked pale. She whispered to Mama, but I could hear her.

'Mama, it's my turn.'

'Your turn at what, dear?'

'Mama, my *turn*. I need a napkin—I'm bleeding.'

'But you're not due until next week.'

'I know Mama. I'm scared.'

They left the parlour together and I knew better than to follow them.

As we went to bed, Freddy still looked pale and very tired, but Mama said he didn't have a fever, so a good night's sleep would soon have him better. It was decided I should sleep in Mama and Papa's room.

As I passed our room, I heard Freddy say: "I tell you Betty, there was dried blood on a couple of those slides." I was going to go in and ask more, but Papa came upstairs and said I should go to bed.

The next morning, Freddy came down for breakfast looking much better, but Betty declared she felt weak and couldn't leave bed, and please may she have her breakfast upstairs. Mama reluctantly agreed, though we all thought she was well enough to come downstairs.

As we finished breakfast there was a knock on the front door. Papa answered it and I peered round his side to see who it was.

There was a carrier, with his horse and cart. The horse kept shifting in its harness and pawing the ground, and shaking its head and snorting.

'Can I give the horse an apple, Papa?'

'Best not, miss,' said the carrier. 'I don't know what's wrong with her today, but she's been acting very jittery. Here guv'nor, this is for you.'

He handed Papa a portable chest of drawers. I could see it was a set of slides for the projector, but rather than varnished wood, this chest was all black. It must have been old as there were dark red stains on it.

'What is it, Papa? Is it the missing slides?'

'We'll see, Cassie.'

Mama had to go to the music hall to work, but Papa said I could stay at home and look after Betty. When Betty heard this, she said all she needed was to rest and perhaps a little light lunch, brought up on a tray. I heard her tell Mama that her turn had stopped.

Betty did stay in bed, but Papa said I wasn't to take up a tray. If she was hungry enough, she'd come downstairs, otherwise she would be sleeping and best to leave her.

Freddy and Papa spent the morning looking at the new slides from the black chest of drawers. Freddy was excited, as this was the set he'd been looking for—the set Havant had been working on for Halloween.

They held them to the light from the window, to see the images. Some of the slides had levers, so you could animate the image, by moving one piece of glass in front of another.

'They really are gruesome,' said Freddy, as he passed them to Papa.

'Ay lad, but that's what people want at Halloween, something to give them the jitters and collywobbles.'

'What's the story on the slides?' I said.

Papa looked down at me. 'Well, Cassie, that's for Fred to work out. He'll show you later.'

'I don't know Father, some of these images—they may give Cassie nightmares.'

'Nay lad, Cassie knows it's all make believe. Don't you Cassie?'

I nodded solemnly.

'Fred, we need to get families into the show—those ha'pennies we charge for the kids, they soon add up, you know. Here, I have an idea. You work out a story which uses the slides and we'll put on a show for your mother and Cassie this evening. We can set up a sheet over the window for the screen, Betty can extemporise on the piano and I'll make up dialogue as necessary. Lad, don't look so worried. It's not to be perfect; just so we can show your mother we've made some progress. Cassie, run and fetch Betty. Tell her she's to be the star of the new show.'

He caught Freddy's look of puzzlement.

'I know lad, she's only playing the piano, but we'll never get her out of bed else.'

When I'd got Betty up, I returned downstairs. Fred and Papa were still looking at slides from the black chest of drawers. They'd placed half a dozen on the table. I picked one up and held it to the sunlight.

I could make out a girl sitting at a dressing table, who looked a lot like Betty. She was brushing her hair. I wanted to see the next slide in the sequence, but Freddy said I couldn't as that would spoil the surprise.

131

When Betty did come down I went upstairs with my doll, Rebecca, into our room as no-one wanted to answer any questions.

Mother came home at seven o'clock. At supper, I thought Papa, Fred and Betty were quieter than usual and Mama commented on how pale we all looked.

After supper, Mama and I were told to stay in the kitchen, so they could set up the screen and mineral oil lamps in the projector.

When we entered the parlour, the projector was lit and sat on a pile of books on the table to ensure the slides wouldn't have the shadow of Mama's head obscuring them. Betty sat at the piano, Freddy was operating the projector and Papa stood to the right of the screen. There was no slide in the projector and so Papa was illuminated by it. As he would be looking at the light from the projector, I knew he wouldn't actually be able to see us.

'My Lords, Ladies and Gentlemen!' said Papa.

I giggled as there was only Mama and I in the audience.

'Tonight I shall tell you a story of darkness and deadly deeds, of the demise of the Derwent family at the hands of the most monstrous and devilish demon, Mephistophilis, in a tale we call: The Devils Among Us!'

Mama and I both said "oooh!" as Fred pushed the title slide into place. Then by using a brass lens cover he obscured that image and revealed a picture of the Derwent family in their parlour, projected from the other lens. Mr Derwent stood behind his wife, who was sewing in a chair. Their eldest daughter sat at the piano, with her brother standing beside her. The youngest daughter played with a doll on the floor.

Papa told us how, one winter night the wind was howling and the clouds racing across the moon—which Freddy illustrated with a moving slide. He'd showed it to me earlier, how one sheet of glass with clouds painted on it could be slid in front of another with the full moon on it. Betty and Fred made whistling noises like the wind and Papa encouraged Mother and I to join in, and then Betty played some very grave chords on the piano.

'That terrible night,' said Papa, 'Mr Derwent suggested they play an innocent game of shadow puppets.'

The screen showed the son making the shadow of a bunny rabbit in the light from a lantern. The next slide showed only the wall and the circle of light from the Derwent's lantern and the shadow of a dog.

'Ah, if only the lad had stayed with the simple animals we know,' said Papa. 'But he was a mischievous lad, very fond of the penny dreadfuls, with their tales of murders and the Devil's work. He decided to give his family a seasonal shadow as the calendar showed it was 31st October—Halloween! He decided he would show his family the shadow of the Devil himself!'

On the screen, we saw the Derwent's son standing in front of the lamp with his shoulders hunched and his fingers clawed. Behind him, his shadow was on the wall. Jerkily, the shadow of a man with small horns and long spiky fingers rose in a circular motion. I guessed this must be a slide with a lever and a pivot and a second sheet of glass with this new shadow painted on it.

I turned to look at Freddy to see how he was working it. He stood behind the projector, quite still. The light escaping from the chimney on the projector lit his face from below. His eyes had rolled up, so I could only see the whites.

Behind him on the wall was the shadow of the man with horns and long spiky fingers.

'Freddy,' I said. 'Are you alright?'

Betty turned on the piano stool to look at him. The shadow raised his right arm and flattened his palm and spiky fingers, so it looked like a blade. He brought his hand down in a slashing movement and as the tips of the shadow's fingers passed across Betty's throat, a red line appeared. She choked and then blood spurted from the wound.

Mama went to her and I ran to the door to watch, as I was certain Papa would know what to do. I knew Papa would make everything alright.

Papa stepped away from the screen and looked at Betty and Mama, at the shadow demon, at Fred standing so still and then at the projector. He stepped towards it, but the shadow saw him move. The demon stretched out an arm and grasped Papa by the throat. He lifted him off the floor and Papa's legs kicked and danced.

'No!' screamed Mama.

The shadow reached out his other hand and took Mama by the throat too. He raised them so their heads nearly touched the ceiling. They both put their hands to their throats to pull at nothing—only shadow. Still they danced.

I could see the silhouette of the shadow's face, his head was tipped back—silently laughing.

As I looked away from his face, my eyes fell on the projector. I realised that Papa had intended to blow out the lamps in it. I stole forward, fearful the shadow would notice me.

At the table, I reached to open the latches on the side of the projector. My wrist was grabbed by Freddy. I looked up into his face, there was blood dripping from his nose again. I tried to pull my hand free, but I couldn't—he was so much bigger than me.

With my other hand I reached for the latches again, that too was grasped by Freddy. I struggled and kicked him, screaming. Then I put all my effort into pushing and not pulling. That took Freddy off guard and he let go my right hand. I swung at the projector and it toppled to the floor, on the far side of the table from me. Darkness shrouded the room.

I heard my parents' bodies fall. Crawling towards them, I called their names.

The room glowed a flickering yellow and I smelled the spilt oil from the lantern. Near Freddy, the furnishings were quickly on fire. By this light, I stood and looked at my parent's unmoving, glass-eyed faces with sticking out dark tongues.

I turned to look at Freddy, now surrounded by the flames. He did not move and behind him the shadow demon danced and leapt at me.

I ran from the house screaming and into the street. I stood screaming, watching the house which was full ablaze.

They talk about me as if I cannot hear; these men in dark frock coats. They talk about a terrible accident, perhaps my fault, which is why I've made up such a story.

I didn't make this up. I didn't.

My name is Cassandra. Why will no-one believe me?

All they have to do is look at my shadow.

Printed in Great
Britain
by Amazon